The Canyon

The Canyon

By SHEILA COLE

HarperCollins*Publishers*

Library of Congress Cataloging-in-Publication Data
Cole, Sheila.
    The canyon / Sheila Cole.
        p.   cm.
    Summary: Eleven-year-old Zach leads the efforts of his San Diego
community in trying to stop a company from developing the local
canyon that he loves.
    ISBN 0-688-17496-5 — ISBN 0-06-029496-5 (lib. bdg.)
    [1. Canyons—Fiction. 2. Conservation of natural resources—Fiction.
3. Environmental protection—Fiction.   4. Endangered species—Fiction.
5. Perseverance (Ethics)—Fiction.   6. Conduct of life—Fiction.
7. San Diego (Calif.)—Fiction.]   I.Title.
PZ7.C67729 Can   2002   2001039374
[Fic]—dc21   CIP
                                                         AC

Typography by Larissa Lawrynenko
1   2   3   4   5   6   7   8   9   10
❖
First Edition

To the memory of
Lothrop, Lee & Shepard
publisher and haven

ACKNOWLEDGMENTS

I would especially like to thank my editor, Melanie Donovan. Without her belief in this book and her patient editorial goading, I might never have finished it. I would also like to thank Susan Pearson and Jennifer Flannery for their support with this project; Jackie Ogburn, Jonathan Case, and the Committee to Save Homewood Canyon for getting me going; Sasha Cole, who gave me lots of ideas along the way; Avi Mosher, for reminding me about baseball cards; my writing buddies Jean Ferris, Kathy Krull, and Larry Dane Brimner for their companionship; and my husband, Michael Cole, for never once suggesting that I would be better off if I spent my time some other way. His good-humored patience during the long days of writing makes it all possible.

The Canyon

CHAPTER 1

THE TELEVISION WAS turned to the channel 8 local news but no one was in the living room watching it when Zach came in. He walked over to turn it off, when Hap Townsend, the anchor, said, "And now a report about San Ramon Canyon." Zach's hand froze. He had just come from there! The scene on the screen changed and there was the canyon, just as he'd left it a few minutes ago. The voice-over said that the City of San Ramon had given the Bowen Development Corporation permission to build a gated community with ninety-five luxury homes in the canyon.

Zach wasn't sure that he had heard right. A housing development in San Ramon Canyon? Everybody in San Ramon went to the canyon. It was where they went to run, walk, watch birds, climb rocks, or just hang out. Zach rushed into the kitchen, calling "Mom! They're going to put a development in the canyon! It was on the news."

His mother was speaking on the telephone. She put her

hand over the receiver and said to Zach, "What's that on your shirt?"

Zach looked down at the tiny black pellets that were clinging to his shirt and absently brushed them away.

"Stop! You're getting it all over the floor. Take your shirt off outside and leave it there," she told him. "The stuff is probably on your jeans and socks, too."

"Mom, they're going to build houses in—," he tried again to tell her, but she wasn't listening. She had returned to her phone conversation.

Zach went out to the backyard and took off his shirt, carefully lifting it over his head with his eyes squeezed shut. He could feel the pellets catching in his hair and sliding down his face. He took off his jeans and shook them, then removed his shoes and socks. He left the clothes on the patio and came inside in his underpants. He shuddered and decided to shower. He washed his hair twice, using lots of shampoo.

When he came back to the kitchen, his father was home from the lab. He was washing lettuce for the salad. His mother was at her usual post in front of the stove. There was the sound of scraping and squawking coming from the den, where his brother was practicing the violin.

"Zach, didn't you say they're going to build houses in the canyon?" Mom asked.

"Where did you hear that?" Dad asked.

"On the channel eight news," Zach replied, snatching a carrot from the cutting board.

"Are you sure they were talking about San Ramon Canyon?"

Zach nodded.

"I heard that the city was planning to buy that land for a park. They wouldn't have given someone permission to build," Mom said.

"But Mom, the reporter said the city gave them a permit," Zach insisted.

"That's too bad. I'm sorry to hear it," Mom said, as Zach's sister, Lucy, walked in.

"What's too bad?" Lucy asked, looking around at everybody.

"They are going to build a bunch of houses in the canyon," Zach told her.

"That's terrible. Who told you that?" said Lucy. Suddenly she started to cry. It seemed to Zach that these days Lucy burst into tears at the least provocation. But this time, he thought she had a good reason to cry.

"Somebody has to stop them. It's the only nice place around here, except for the mall!" she wailed.

"What do you want us to do about it, honey?" Mom asked. "The city has already given them a permit to build. Zach heard it on the news."

"I don't know—," she blubbered miserably. "Something. Protest. Sit in. Lie down in front of the bulldozers. Something."

Dad reached over and put his arm around Lucy's shoulders

and pulled her to him in a hug, saying, "Come on, Princess, don't be so sad."

This was too much for Zach. He headed for the den. Ben's violin was better than this. Besides, all the talk about the canyon reminded him that he had worries of his own.

"Hey, Ben, do you know what bat poop looks like?"

Ben put down his violin. "What?"

"Do you know what bat poop looks like?" Zach repeated.

"Why are you asking?"

"Just wondering."

"You can look it up on the Web. You can find out about everything on there," Ben replied. "Even bat poop." Nine years old and already a budding computer geek, Ben spent hours on-line. Zach thought it was unhealthy for Ben to spend all of that time sitting in front of a computer screen, but his parents didn't see anything wrong with it. He had overheard his mom tell his grandmother Suni that Ben was "very bright" and that Lucy was, too. But she said Zach was "not fulfilling his potential." That had made Zach feel bad, even though he didn't know what his potential was or how he might fulfill it.

"Bats eat insects but I don't know what their poop looks like. Ask Uncle Dave. He'll know. He used to be a caver," Ben said.

"A what?" Zach asked.

"A person who explores caves," Ben answered.

"I didn't know he did that. That's cool," Zach said, before

he realized his mother was standing in the doorway.

"Is that where you picked up all of those little black pellets?" she asked. "Zach, you know you're not supposed to go in caves."

Zach swung around to face her, shaking his head no. "They're probably from Trevor's garage," he lied. "I was helping him look for his dad's baseball cards."

After dinner Zach asked Ben to help him look up bats. They were just printing out all the information they had found when Trevor called. He wanted to know if Zach could come with him to the baseball card show on Sunday.

"Sure, but I have to ask— Hey!" Zach said, "I looked up bats on the Internet. There are lots of different kinds in San Diego."

"So?" Trevor asked as if he didn't know why Zach was saying this.

"If there was a bat in the cave we were in, it was probably a little brown myotis or a California myotis—those are the kinds that live around here," Zach told him.

"Just because there are bats in San Diego, doesn't mean that one flew into you, Zach. There were no bats in there, only mice."

"It was a bat. If you want, we can go back with flashlights and I'll show them to you," said Zach.

Trevor laughed. "There's no way I'm going back in that cave with you, dude. You practically stomped me trying to get out of there."

"It was sort of scary, but that was because you couldn't see anything," Zach was telling his friends Brian Nocon and Robert Berman about the cave the next day. The boys were standing on the school playground at lunchtime.

"Didn't you have a flashlight?" asked Brian.

Zach shook his head. "We didn't know that we were going to go in. Next time, I'll bring one. Do you want to come?"

"Where?" Trevor asked, joining the group.

"He wants to take us to see this cave," Brian answered.

Trevor hooted with laughter. "Zach? Wants to take you to the cave? You should have heard him. 'Help! Help!'" he said in a high voice. "'Get me out of here!' He sounded like a girl."

"Shut up, Trev. It isn't funny. A bat flew into me," said Zach.

"You doofus, you imagined it," Trevor said, still laughing.

Zach ignored him. "Do you want to come?"

Brian shook his head no.

Trevor poked him in the shoulder, "Afraid of an imaginary bat flying in your hair? Or maybe you're afraid of being attacked by a mouse? There were mice in there."

"Lay off, Trev," said Robert. "Hey, Zach, did those pictures you took for that photography contest come out okay?"

Zach sighed. "Yeah, they were okay. But none of them were spectacular. I want to try to get some better ones."

"What contest?" Brian asked.

"*Natural History* is having this junior wildlife photography contest. First prize is a hundred fifty dollars," Zach said.

"Wow! One hundred and fifty bucks! That'll buy a lot of baseball cards," Brian said.

Zach smiled. "That's the idea."

Robert laughed. "Take Trevor's picture. He's a wild animal." He hooted, imitating an ape. Brian and Trevor joined him, hooting and leaning forward with their arms dangling like apes.

Zach laughed with them.

It was not until he was lying in bed thinking about the day's events that it occurred to Zach that he didn't need a witness to prove that the cave had bats in it. He could take a picture of them. That is, if his camera was okay. His mouth went dry as he remembered dropping the Nikon on a narrow ledge while shooting pictures for the contest. An inch to the right and it would have fallen a hundred feet to the canyon floor and been smashed beyond repair. It was no cheap point-and-shoot camera. It was the kind good photographers use and it had been his grandfather's. Aside from his collection of baseball cards, it was Zach's most precious possession, and he had completely forgotten to clean the lens. He got out of bed. Quietly, so as not to wake up Ben, he fumbled around in the dark until he found his camera bag. He took the bag and tiptoed into the bathroom with it. He turned on the light and examined the lens for scratches. Surprisingly, there weren't any. He took the lens off and cleaned it gently. Tomorrow was Saturday and he was going back to that cave to prove that there were bats in there.

Ben was already at the computer in his pajamas when Zach got up on Saturday morning. Lucy and Dad were out riding their bikes and Mom was still asleep. "Hey, Ben," Zach said, coming up behind him. "I need you to do something for me." Ben turned to him with a what-do-you-want-now look on his face. "But you have to promise you won't tell Mom and Dad," Zach continued and Ben's expression changed to one of interest. "I want you to hold the lights for me while I take some pictures of the bats in this cave we discovered."

Ben was excited about the cave, and when he became excited about anything, he talked about it endlessly. "Do you know, Zach, that there's this cave called Carlsbad Caverns and it's the deepest limestone cave in the entire United States? I read about it in a magazine. It is 1,567 feet deep and over half a million Mexican freetail bats live in it. It takes twenty minutes for the whole colony to leave the cave in the evening when they go out to feed. People have timed it. I want to go there."

"I don't want to disappoint you, Ben," Zach said, "but this cave isn't like that. It's small and it isn't limestone. And if you keep talking about caves, you are going to make Mom think something's up. I've got to go to soccer. Be ready when I get home. Okay?"

Zach couldn't believe it. Ben was still in his pajamas playing a game on the computer when he came home from his soccer game. "Come on, Ben, get dressed," Zach said. "Concentrate!" Ben had a tendency to daydream and forget what he was doing.

Finally, they were out of the house. They walked up Canyon Road, past Trevor's house. At the top of the hill, they turned onto Crest Drive and followed it until they came to the path that led down into the canyon. Halfway down the bluff, they veered off the path and cut through the chaparral to the cave. "This is it," Zach said.

Ben looked at the opening doubtfully. Even though Zach had warned him it was small, he had imagined a grand archway leading into a cave as big as a palace, like the one in his favorite video game, Wizard Quest. This was just a dark gash in the side of the cliff, too low for anything taller than a cocker spaniel to walk into.

"You have to get down on your stomach," Zach said. "Follow me!" He crawled into the entrance. Inside the cave, the air was cold. Only a few feet from the entrance it was dark enough that Zach couldn't see the narrow walls and low roof, but he felt them closing in around him. He could barely breathe. A few more feet and it was so dark he thought he might have closed his eyes. He blinked to make sure he hadn't. Then he opened them as wide as he could. He couldn't see a thing. He strained to pick up every sound. He could hear the scuffle of Ben's shoes coming from outside the cave. He crept forward a little more and was hit by a sharp smell. "Ben, are you coming?" he called.

9

"It's cold in here," Ben said, dragging himself into the cave. "They say it is always fifty-six degrees in Carlsbad Caverns, no matter what the temperature is outside. What do you think the temperature is in here, Zach?"

"I don't know," Zach said, inching along. "Can you hold the flashlight higher?"

"It's hard when I'm crawling like this," Ben complained, and then stopped. "What's that smell?"

Zach wasn't listening. He was peering at the cave walls, searching for bats—afraid that he might miss them in the flashlight's dim light.

As they went deeper into the cave and he still didn't see any sign of the bats, Zach started to worry that he wouldn't find them and he would have to endure Trevor's teasing again. Ben was still going on and on, reeling off bat facts that he had gotten from the Internet.

"Shut up, Ben!" Zach snapped. "I can't hear anything with your nonstop talking. Point the flashlight up." Ben subsided into a hurt silence and moved the flashlight beam up the cave wall to the ceiling.

There they were—a whole lot of bats, shrieking at them from above. They looked like extraterrestrials in a movie, with their sharp-toothed mouths wide open, their huge antennalike ears, and their skin wings. It was all Zach could do to keep himself from backing out of the cave as fast as he could, but he forced himself to stay and look at them.

"Wow!" Ben yelled.

"Shh! You'll scare them away," Zach said firmly. "Hold the flashlight steady so I can take some pictures." He reached behind, unzipped his backpack, and pulled out his camera. He was afraid that the flash would startle the bats so he worked quickly. As he did, his fear was replaced by fascination. Hugging the cave walls and chirping in terror, the bats reminded him of some baby birds he had once seen trying to scare off a bigger bird. He only quit shooting when the roll of film was finished.

"That was awesome," Ben said as they were backing out of the cave.

Zach agreed. It *was* awesome.

Afterward, Ben had to go home to practice the violin before his lesson, but Zach lingered in the canyon. He wanted to take some more pictures for the *Natural History* contest. He reloaded the camera with faster film and started to wander through the canyon, looking for things to photograph. There were so many places to look that he didn't know where to begin. There was the magnificent stand of eucalyptus near the top of the canyon where horned owls liked to roost. There were the tan and red bluffs where coyotes and bobcats had their dens hidden among the bushes of the chaparral. There were the reeds at the edge of the creek, which looked golden in the sunlight. He might find a raccoon lurking there. And there was the creek itself, a sparkling chain among the gray boulders. There were always birds flitting around there.

He headed toward the creek, stopping along the way to

take a picture of a rabbit crouched under a black sage. He took another one of a blue heron standing in the creek. Then he climbed up a bluff. He noticed a round hole surrounded by freshly dug dirt. He wondered what animal had made the hole. Then his mind wandered to the animals that lived in the canyon and where they would go if the news report he had heard was right. In his mind he saw the bulldozers clearing the hillsides, pushing a stampede of animals before them. He was distracted from his thoughts by a shadow and looked up to see a red-tailed hawk circling him as if he were prey. Zach rolled on his back and took a picture of the hawk. The hawk flew off and Zach settled back to watch the hole.

He had just about decided to leave when there was a blur in front of his eyes and he pressed the shutter on the camera before he even knew what he was seeing. The click of the shutter made the animal disappear back into its hole. Zach got up. It was probably a wasted shot, but it didn't matter—he had plenty of film. Most important, he had the bat pictures to show Trevor. Maybe they would be good enough to enter in the *Natural History* contest.

CHAPTER 2

ZACH STEPPED INTO THE house and came face-to-face with his mother. "What do you think you were doing, taking your brother into that cave?" she demanded. Without giving him a chance to answer, she went on, "You know that those caves are dangerous. They collapse all the time."

Zach peered around his mother. Ben was standing a few feet behind her, sheepishly brushing his shirt with his hand. Zach looked down at his own T-shirt. It, too, was covered with telltale black pellets.

Seeing that he couldn't deny her accusations, Zach tried to bring a quick end to his mother's tirade. "Mom, Mom," he said, "it's dangerous. I know. I'm sorry we went. We won't do it again. Okay?"

But his mother kept going. "How can I trust you when you do something like that? And you lied to me! I don't want you ever doing that again. Do you hear me, Zachary? I have

13

half a mind to make the canyon off-limits altogether."

"It doesn't matter anyway. I won't be able to go there after they build that development," he responded under his breath as he walked out to the backyard to take his clothes off. He couldn't understand how grown-ups could let this happen. It was like watching someone commit a crime, because it was a crime to clear the canyon and put a bunch of houses down there, Zach thought.

As soon as he showered and changed his clothes, Zach rode his bike to the one-hour photo shop on San Ramon Boulevard. He filled out two envelopes, placed one roll of film in each and handed them to the clerk. The clerk said the pictures would be ready to pick up after school on Monday.

On school days, Zach and Trevor met at the end of Zach's driveway and walked to school together. Ben walked ahead by himself so he could get to school in time to play four-square with his friends. But on this Monday morning Zach asked Ben to wait with him and be his witness that they had seen bats in the cave. They sat on the front steps and waited, and then waited some more, but Trevor did not come. Ten minutes before the bell, they ran down the hill to school without him. Zach slid into his seat just as the bell rang and turned around to look for Trevor. His seat was empty. Where was he?

As soon as Zach got home, he picked up the telephone and dialed Trevor's house.

Trevor's mother answered the phone. She said Trevor was sleeping. He had a cold and he wouldn't be at school tomorrow, either. She asked Zach to bring Trevor his homework after school the next day.

Well, Zach thought, he'd bring Trevor more than homework. He smiled as he headed out the door. Zach rode his bike down the hill to the photo shop. He handed in his claim stubs and waited impatiently while the clerk flipped through a stack of envelopes. He paid the man and excitedly slid the photographs out of the first envelope. The first photograph was all black. He didn't think much of it because it wasn't unusual for the first photograph on a roll not to come out. He peeled it off and saw that the second one was black too, and his breath caught. The third one was also black, and so was the fourth. Everything became blurry as he flipped through one black photograph after another—eighteen in all. Then he came to a shadowy picture. He wiped his eyes on his sleeve and examined it carefully. There in the shadows was a darker patch against tan, which must have been the bats. The next photo was mostly gray, but if you looked closely, you could see something dark, which must have been the bats. All the rest of the pictures on that roll of film were black. He didn't have the heart to open the second envelope.

"How did they come out?" Ben asked as soon as Zach walked in the door.

"None of the ones we took in the cave came out," Zach

15

said, dropping both envelopes on the counter.

Ben slipped the photographs out of the first envelope. He flipped through the photographs, shaking his head. "They're all black."

Zach nodded. "Good thing Trev wasn't here to see them. He'd never let me live it down."

Zach went straight to Trevor's house after school the next afternoon. Trevor answered the door in his pajamas. "Do you want to come in?" he asked. "I don't have a temperature anymore," he added, seeing Zach's doubtful look.

Trevor led the way into the living room and plopped down on the couch. Zach took a chair opposite him.

"I hate being sick. What's happening?" Trevor asked.

"You know the cave?" Zach asked, ready to tell him about seeing the bats.

"Where you were attacked by a mouse?" He laughed and started to cough.

"It was a bat. I went back with a flashlight and saw lots of them. I tried to take pictures, but they didn't come out."

Trevor shrugged.

"It was a bat," Zach insisted.

"Whatever," Trevor said. "Tell you what, I'm going to school tomorrow. If you want, you can show me. Okay? Do you want to see the new baseball cards my mom bought me?" He got off the couch and led Zach through the house to his bedroom, where he kept his collection of baseball cards.

Trevor was most proud of his new Carlos Delgado card,

16

but the card Zach most envied was his Brian Sikorski rookie card. He would have given a lot to be able to trade Trevor for it. The problem was that he didn't have any cards that Trevor wanted. He wished his mother would buy him baseball cards when he was sick, like Trevor's mother did.

CHAPTER 3

AS ZACH OPENED HIS FRONT door after school he heard the tinkling sounds of the piano. Good, his mother was giving a lesson. She would take one look at him and know he was up to something. Zach hurried to his room; he needed to be out of the house before the lesson ended.

Remembering the telltale black pellets from his visits to the cave and his mother's threat to make the canyon off limits, Zach searched for something to put on over his jeans and shirt that he could take off before he came home. Finding an old stretched-out shirt was easy, but none of his jeans were big enough to go over the ones he was wearing. In desperation he looked in Lucy's room. There, lying in a heap of clothes on the floor, was a pair of purple sweat pants. He picked them up and slipped them on over his own pants.

Zach was walking out the door when his sister came up the stairs.

"Are those my sweats?" she demanded.

"Sh!" Zach whispered. "I'll bring them back. It's an emergency," and he tore down the stairs and down the walk with her yelling after him, "You little creep. They're my favorite sweats. Take them off!"

Zach ran up the street. Trevor was waiting at the corner. He started to laugh as soon as he saw Zach. "Hey, dude, that your special bat cave uniform? Who are you? Super Zach?"

"Yup," said Zach. "This is my super protective covering for bat poop."

"Where'd you get those purple pants, bat boy? They're hot."

"Like them? Got them special," he said holding them out like a girl with a skirt.

Trevor rolled his eyes. "They're Lucy's?" he guessed.

"What do you want?" Zach asked. "A fashion show? They fit, don't they? The bats aren't going to care."

"O-o-o-o-oh, touchy, touchy!" Trevor said, wagging his finger in a tsk-tsk motion.

Zach turned and started walking quickly with Trevor right behind him. He broke into a run as they turned down the path to the canyon. Racing around a bend in the path, Zach nearly collided with a jogger coming up the bluff toward them. He jumped aside to let the jogger pass and noticed a pink plastic streamer fluttering amid the dark green of the bushes at his feet. It was tied to a wooden stake about two feet high. Looking out across the chaparral, he saw that there were dozens of stakes with streamers attached.

"Hey, mister," Trevor called to the jogger. "What are those pink ribbons for?"

The jogger turned around to answer and ran in place. "They're some kind of marker. Either for surveying or for grading. They're for the development. I'm going to miss this place." He waved as he ran off up the path.

Trevor turned to Zach. "What development?"

"Didn't you hear? The Bowen Corporation is going to close the canyon and build a housing development. Can you believe it?" Zach replied.

Trevor was outraged. "They can't do that," he said. "This is our canyon!"

"No, it isn't. It belongs to the Bowen Corporation and they're developing it," said Zach.

"But they can't—a whole canyon? Somebody should . . . ," Trevor sputtered.

"Do something," Zach finished his sentence. "The city gave them a permit. It was on the news."

"So they're going to let them bulldoze our canyon?" Trevor asked.

Zach nodded. "I wish we could stop them."

Trevor nodded. He took a deep breath and let it out slowly as he gazed out over the canyon. Suddenly he pulled himself up so he was standing tall. His green eyes glittered with excitement. "We can!" he said.

"Can what?" Zach asked.

"Sabotage them," Trevor said. He waved his arm in the

direction of the stakes. "We'll pull these up so they won't know where anything is supposed to go."

Trevor's excitement was contagious. In a matter of seconds, Zach's flashlight was lying in the dirt alongside his backpack and he was threading his way through the brush to the nearest stake. He put his hands around it, ready to yank it up, and hesitated. Trevor jumped in front of him, brandishing a stake in each hand. "Come on, man! Let's go!"

Zach's face went hot and then cold. He clenched his jaw and yanked the stake out of the ground, tossed it in the air, and turned to scan the bluff for another one. He glanced back to see if Trevor was watching, but Trevor had disappeared. He reached down for the second stake and drew it out of the ground. As he was standing up he thought he saw somebody move higher up the bluff. But when he looked around a moment later, no one was there. It was just Trevor, he thought as he went on to the next stake. This one was wedged deep into the earth and Zach nearly fell into a patch of spiny cactus trying to dislodge it. After that, it got easy. He bent over, grabbed a stake, pulled it out, and dropped it mechanically. It was as if he were in a trance, yanking up one stake, then another, and then another.

He stopped only when he couldn't see any more pink ribbons fluttering in the breeze. He realized with a shiver that he had better hurry home if he didn't want to have to answer a lot of questions. He looked around for Trevor but didn't see him. "Trevor!" he called. There was no answer. He couldn't leave without Trevor.

Suddenly he felt a sharp slap on the back. He swung his head around. Trevor was standing behind him with a grin on his face. "We did it!" he said triumphantly. "We pulled them all up!"

"Yeh, we did," Zach said as they climbed up the bluff together.

"Next," Trevor said, "we'll dig pits for the bulldozers to fall in. We'll disconnect their truck batteries."

"And we'll steal their spark plugs," Zach added, getting caught up in Trevor's excitement.

"We'll put sand in their gas tanks," Trevor continued.

"And we'll steal their lumber and hide it somewhere so they can't find it," Zach went on.

"It's our canyon and nobody's going to take it away," said Trevor.

"This is a job for Super Zach and his faithful companion, Trevor the Revenger!" Zach shouted, shooting his fist over his head.

Trevor held his fist in the air, too, shouting, "We rule!"

Zach opened the door to his house and heard Lucy's voice and then his father's coming from the kitchen and the sound of spoons scraping against plates.

"Is that you, Zach?" his father called.

"Sorry I'm late," Zach said as he slipped into his place at the table without meeting anybody's eyes. "I forgot what time it was." He picked up his soup spoon.

"You may be late, Zach, but that's no excuse for not washing your hands. Go wash them," Mom ordered.

Zach stood up. "Those *are* my pants!" said Lucy. "I thought they were. Take them off this minute, you little creep!"

Zach had forgotten that he was wearing his sister's purple sweats. "Sorry, Luce," he said, starting to slide them off.

"We're eating. Don't take those things off in here. They're filthy," Mom said.

Zach washed his hands and quickly returned to the table. He dipped his spoon into the vegetable soup and was just bringing it to his mouth when his mother asked, "So what were you doing that was so important that you forgot what time it was? You had us worried."

"Nothing," Zach said, not meeting his mother's eyes.

"You have a watch, next time use it," his mother said. Then she turned to ask Lucy about her day.

Zach ate his soup and listened while Lucy told them about a girl at her school who had been caught shoplifting a silver necklace at Target and had to go before a juvenile judge. "They let her go with a warning, but Bethany says that next time they'll send her to the Girls' Rehabilitation Center."

"What's that?" Ben asked.

"It's a reform school where they send kids who break the law," Dad explained.

Zach wondered if they sent kids there for pulling up surveyors' stakes. He wasn't hungry anymore.

CHAPTER 4

AT FIRST, ZACH COULDN'T stop worrying that someone had seen them in the canyon. He kept imagining
that Trevor and he were in a reform school, defend-
ing each other against gangs and drug lords. But as days went
by and nothing happened, he stopped thinking about it. He
had other things on his mind, like the report he was writing
for science on bats and echolocation, which was due on
Wednesday.

He was standing at the kitchen counter looking through
the photographs of the bats, hoping they might inspire him to
write his report. They were still all black. Zach sighed. Seeing
him with the photographs, his mom asked if they were the
ones he took for the *Natural History* contest.

"These didn't turn out," Zach replied, stuffing them back
into the envelope before she saw that they were pictures of
bats and remembered that he had gone in a cave.

"What about these?" she said, picking up the other envelope of pictures. She slipped the photographs out of the

envelope and flipped through them. "What's the matter with this one?" she asked, holding out the photograph of the blue heron for Zach to see. "It's a terrific picture."

"Pictures! Let me see," Lucy said, coming into the kitchen dressed in white for her karate class. She looked over her mother's shoulder at the photograph. "Ooh! I like the heron! What's this one? It's so cute," Lucy said, holding a picture of a mouse.

So that's what made that hole, Zach thought. He sighed impatiently. "Can't you see? It's a mouse."

"Look at its little eyes," Lucy cooed. "They look like apple seeds. Can I put it up on the fridge?"

"Sure," Zach agreed, surprised himself at how good the photo was.

"Lucy, you are going to be late for your karate class if you don't go," Mom reminded her.

Lucy glanced at the clock on the wall and dashed out the door.

Zach sat down to work on his report again. Maybe he could add a section on vampire bats. It made his spine tingle just thinking about how they snuck up on their sleeping victims and bit into them and lapped up the blood with their tongues like cats lapping milk. But lapping up blood didn't have anything to do with how bats get around by hearing their echoes. Maybe he should try to take some more pictures. No, that wouldn't help either. What he really needed was some fresh air.

He got up from the table and went into his parents' bedroom. He picked up the telephone and dialed Trevor's number. "Hey Trev, still want to see the bats?"

"Sure," Trevor said.

"Meet me at the path in ten," Zach said and hung up.

On his way to the canyon, Zach saw Brian riding his bike down the street. "Hey, Brian," he yelled, "Trev and I are going to the canyon. Do you want to come?"

"You can't go down there. Didn't you hear? The canyon is closed," Brian called. "We tried to go yesterday and there was a fence around it."

"You're kidding," Zach said. "They can't do that. . . . It's . . . it's . . . ," he sputtered. "Are you sure?"

"Go see for yourself," said Brian.

Sure enough, when Zach reached the path, there was Trevor standing by a nine-foot-high chain-link fence blocking the entrance. Attached to the fence was a sign that said:

NO TRESPASSING

PRIVATE PROPERTY

TRESPASSERS WILL BE PROSECUTED

Through the fence, they could see a new crop of bright pink plastic ribbons amid the dark green of the sage and sumac bushes.

"They might think that this thing is going to keep me out,

but it's not," Trevor said. He backed up and ran at the fence and jumped, but he failed to clear the top and fell to the ground. He backed up and tried again and again, but the fence was too high for him to jump. Both Zach and Trevor tried to climb it, but the links were too fine to get finger- or toeholds.

"We could go through Klapper's backyard," Trevor suggested. Everybody in the neighborhood knew that you could get to the canyon through Old Man Klapper's backyard but few used it. Mr. Klapper had a reputation as a mean old guy and his dog's was worse. Balls that fell in his yard lay unclaimed if Rogue was loose. It was said that cats that crossed the Rottweiler's path were never seen again.

Zach's eyes widened in disbelief. "Are you crazy?"

"The only way in now is through Old Man Klapper's backyard."

"What about Rogue? There's no way. I'm not going in that yard," Zach said.

"Not even if the dog's locked up?"

"Old Man Klapper will let him out."

"He might not be home."

"How are we going to know?"

"Look, here's a pinecone. We'll pretend we're playing catch and I'll throw a fastball at his front door. If Old Man Klapper is home, he'll come out and yell at us like he always does. And if Rogue comes to get the pinecone, we'll give up. If the dog doesn't come, we go in."

27

"Okay," Zach said reluctantly. "But if either of them show, I'm out of here."

"Let's play ball."

Trevor and Zach threw the pinecone back and forth, edging closer and closer to Klapper's yard. On the fifth round, Trevor suddenly pivoted so he was directly facing the door and threw a fast ball at it. Both of the boys tensed, ready to run for their lives. As soon as the pinecone hit the door, it triggered a barrage of furious barking. Zach saw Rogue's jowly face pressed against the picture window, looking to see who was invading his territory. His saliva splattered the window as he barked, but the front door remained closed.

"Go!" Trevor said, jumping the fence and running along the side of Mr. Klapper's house. Zach was right behind him. There was a closed gate behind the house. Trevor pulled the latchstring. The gate swung open. The boys scrambled down the bluff into the canyon. They were panting and out of breath by the time they came to a stop. Trevor looked at Zach and grinned. "It worked!"

"Good thing. Otherwise we'd be dog food," Zach said with a grin.

"You were scared witless. You should have seen yourself."

"You are such a jerk, Trev," Zach said, turning from him to look across the canyon at the facing cliff, which had eroded into a series of vertical ridges. Lower down, where the incline was not so steep, the cliff was covered with the dark bushes of the chaparral. At the bottom of the canyon was a thin thread of water that became a roaring creek after it rained. It was beautiful. Zach could understand why someone would want to live here. As he scanned the bluffs, Zach saw a white truck parked close to the fence. What was that doing there? He stared at it for a few seconds, to make sure no one was inside. He felt a poke in his rib.

Trevor was standing like a fencer, with a surveyor's stake in Zach's side. "*En garde!*" Trevor said. "Do we pull ze stakes, or must I run you through with my trusted sword?"

"I'm pulling, I'm pulling," said Zach, bending down to grab hold of a stake. He tugged at it until it came out of the ground. He let go of it, then straightened up and scanned the hillside for another stake. He did this again and again, until his back and arm ached and his hand was full of splinters and there was a blister forming on the palm of his hand and another one on his thumb. He was hot and thirsty and he wanted to go to the bathroom, but he made himself go on. "It's for the canyon," he told himself each time he pulled up a stake.

The sun sank behind the cliffs and the canyon was left in shadow. Zach looked at his watch. It was six 'clock, time to leave if he didn't want to catch it. "Hey, Trev, I got to go!" he yelled. Old Man Klapper would be coming home any moment. He might already be there. He pictured Rogue's slobbering jaws pressed against the window. "Trevor!" he yelled.

"I'm here," Trevor called from off to the right. "Last one to the gate is a rotten egg."

Zach climbed up to the edge of Mr. Klapper's property. Trevor had beaten him there and was opening the gate. It gave a loud creak and in a flash Rogue appeared at the sliding glass doors that opened onto the patio. It was a good thing it was closed now. Rogue threw himself at the glass and let out a bloodcurdling howl as the boys passed the windows, rounded the corner of the house, and scrambled over the fence.

They didn't stop running until they came to Trevor's house. Trevor threw himself against his mother's SUV, which was parked in the driveway, and exhaled. A second later Zach threw himself beside Trevor. They leaned against the back bumper, panting, then turned to smile at one another. Just then a battered truck chugged up the hill past them and turned into Mr. Klapper's driveway. They burst out laughing.

CHAPTER 5

"YOU KNOW, TREV, I've been thinking," Zach said as they walked home from school the next day. Ben was up ahead chattering away to a boy from his class. "We pulled up the stakes yesterday and the Bowen Corporation will probably put them back again tomorrow and then we'll pull them up again and then they'll put them back."

"Yeah, but as long as we keep pulling them up, they can't bring in the bulldozers," Trevor replied.

Zach shook his head. "Think, Trev. There's that fence. Nobody can go in the canyon. We have to think of something that will make them take the fence down."

"You're right. We need to do something big—really big." Trevor paused to think of what that could be. His eyes lit up. "We'll make a bomb and put it under one of their earth-movers and it will blow up. *POW! POW!* The metal will fly all over the place, mowing everybody down. We'll dig booby traps and put sharp poisoned sticks in them so when the guys

31

who are working on the development fall into them they'll die. We'll catch some rattlers and hide them in their earth-movers. We'll . . ."

"I'm not blowing up anything," Zach said firmly.

Trevor's jaw dropped. "But—but you were the one who said we had to do something."

"I did," Zach said, "but I don't want to hurt anybody."

"So how are we going to stop them?" Trevor asked.

Zach shrugged his shoulders. He couldn't think of anything. Except . . . maybe. No, he knew what Trevor would say. Better not to mention it.

"So? Do you want to save the canyon or do you want to stand there and suck your thumb like a baby?" said Trevor. "I'm digging a booby trap."

"I'm in this too, all the way, and you know it, Trevor," Zach said quietly.

Trevor stuck his chin out. "Prove it."

"I don't have to prove anything."

"So are you going to help me dig, or what?" Trevor demanded.

Zach swung his dad's pickax again and again against the side of the cliff. He knew digging a booby trap was wrong, but he couldn't bear to let Trevor think he didn't care about the canyon. He had even gone so far as to take his dad's pick and shovel from the garage without asking. Talk about guilt! And one little hole in this big place wasn't going to change anything.

Nobody would notice it. They'd have to dig hundreds of holes to do any real damage.

He imagined all of the kids he knew digging and smiled to himself. If all of them worked together they really might be able to do something to stop the Bowen Corporation. If only he could think of some other way to stop them, then he could quit digging a stupid booby trap.

Zach stopped swinging the pick and waited as Trevor shoveled the dirt he had loosened to one side. As soon as Trevor finished, Zach started swinging the pick again. It hadn't rained in San Ramon for seven months and the ground was rock hard. Each time Zach swung the pick it bounced off the parched earth, barely leaving a dent.

"My arms are tired. You take a turn," Zach said. He gave the pick to Trevor and wiped his stinging eyes with the hem of his T-shirt. It came away drenched in sweat. He was desperately thirsty, but they hadn't thought to bring anything to drink. He watched as Trevor swung the pick and, when he stopped, Zach shoveled away the loosened dirt. After a half an hour, Trevor stopped and stood up straight. "What do you think?" he asked, looking down at the hole.

"What do you think?" Zach asked him.

"I think we'll never get anywhere at this rate," Trevor said.

Zach shrugged his shoulders. "What do you want to do?"

"Why do I always have to be the one who says what we're going to do?" Trevor said.

Zach swallowed hard. He didn't know what to say. Then his face brightened. "I saw a truck parked up by the fence yesterday. We could let the air out of its tires. If it's still there."

"You're the man, Zach! Let's do it," Trevor said, dropping the pick in the hole.

"We can't leave my dad's tools. He'll kill me," Zach said. Trevor retrieved the pick and followed Zach around the side of the bluff and up to the truck. It had BOWEN DEVELOPMENT CORPORATION printed on the side in big red letters. Trevor lifted the pick over his head and smashed it down into the hood of the truck. "Take that, Bowen!" he snarled.

What was Trevor doing? They were going to let the air out of the tires. Nobody said anything about punching holes in a truck. "Stop! Stop!" Zach yelled. "Tre-v-v-vor."

Trevor slammed the pick into the hood of the truck again and swung around to face Zach.

"You're wrecking it!" Zach gasped.

Trevor spit at the ground. "Duh! Isn't that what we wanted to do?"

"I—but—but—I thought we were just going to . . . ," Zach sputtered.

"What's the difference? It's us against them. We're not going to get a big corporation like Bowen out of the canyon by being nice."

Zach didn't have an answer to that. "There has to be some other way," he protested.

"You chickening out, Zach? Is that it?" Trevor asked, turning back to the truck.

Zach sighed heavily and walked over to a tire and loosened the cap. He heard the hiss of escaping air. I can't do this, he thought.

Trevor shouted triumphantly as the tires went flat and the truck settled into the dirt. He picked up a rock and threw it at the truck. It hit the windshield with a crack and rebounded onto the hood, leaving a starburst crack in the glass on the passenger side. He picked up another rock and threw it, yelling to Zach, "Come on, Zach. Aren't you going to help?"

Zach shook his head no. He picked the pickax off the ground where Trevor had left it and, with the shovel in the other hand, he started slowly up the cliff to Old Man Klapper's yard. He was winded by the time he reached the top. He paused and looked down the bluff behind him. No Trevor.

Mr. Klapper's house was quiet and there were no lights on. Zach stepped into the yard. There was no sign of Rogue. A large orange dangled from an orange tree, catching the late afternoon light. Zach's mouth parched. He was hot, sweaty, and tired. He leaned the shovel and pickax against the tree trunk and reached for the fruit. As his hand closed around the orange, he heard a loud *crack*! Suddenly his back was on fire. Zach let out an earsplitting yelp and spun around, grabbing at his back. Old Man Klapper was standing behind him with a rifle in his hand.

Zach raced back down the cliff as fast as his legs could carry him. *Smack!* He ran right into Trevor. "He shot me! He shot me!" Zach gasped. "He has a shotgun. Am I bleeding?"

"He shot you?" Trevor said numbly.

Zach shook his head. "He shot me in the back. Man, it hurts!" He turned around and raised his T-shirt for Trevor to inspect his back.

"Don't see any blood, but there's this white stuff all over your shirt. It looks like salt." Zach winced as Trevor brushed off his back. Trevor touched his tongue to his fingers. "It *is* salt."

"It burns," Zach whimpered.

"You'll be okay," Trevor said like he knew all about it.

"Okay? With Klapper sitting out there with his gun and his dog waiting for us?"

"He has to go inside sometime."

Zach sank down on his stomach in the dirt. Now he was not only hot, tired, and thirsty, his back burned and itched.

After a minute Trevor lay down beside him. He started to giggle. "You taste like a French fry."

"It's not funny. It hurts," Zach said grumpily.

"You're not Super Zach, you're Salty Zach," Trevor said, still giggling. "Lord of the Fries."

And then Zach was giggling, too. "Ow! Stop! You're making my back hurt," he groaned. After a while, they did stop and lay there in silence.

The light faded away. Soon it would be dinnertime, Zach thought. His mother and father would be worried. He was going to have to think of something to tell them.

Trevor said, "I'm going to tell my mom we were in the canyon and that we were cutting through Old Man Klapper's backyard and his dog took after us. She knows about Rogue. She'll understand. Your mom will too. She knows Klapper." It was as if he'd read Zach's mind.

"Good plan," Zach said. "Let's see if he's gone."

The boys snuck up to the top of the cliff and peeked over the gate. Rogue paced on the patio like a sentry standing guard.

What if Rogue stayed there all night? His parents would be frantic, Zach realized. They might even call the police. Boy, did his back hurt. He wondered if he would have to go to the hospital. Zach's mind filled with sirens and flashing lights. He pushed the image away and turned to look back at the dark outline of the bluffs against the lilac-colored sky. The dark green bushes looked almost black in the waning light. At the very bottom the creek glittered like a fine silver chain. A lump rose in his throat. It was so beautiful and soon it would be gone. He thought of all the things he and Trevor had done in the canyon—the happiness of climbing its steep cliffs and of jumping from rock to rock in the creek. The joy of finding new places, places that seemed as if no one had ever been there before. He even thought of the bat cave with fondness. "Trevor," he said softly.

"What?"

"I've been thinking. Doing things like we've been doing isn't going to work. We need to do something else."

"What? You don't even know, Zach," Trevor said in a hoarse whisper.

Zach didn't answer.

They sat there in silence for several more minutes as the light faded from the sky. Together they peered over the gate at the house. The lights were on and Mr. Klapper was sitting on the couch watching TV with his back to the window. Rogue was nowhere in sight.

"Let's go," Trevor whispered, unlatching the gate.

"The dog," Zach reminded him. He picked up a pebble and threw it hard against the concrete of the patio. Except for a warning bark from inside the house, nothing happened. Silently, the boys snuck across the yard and out the gate to the street.

CHAPTER 6

"ZACHARY? IS THAT YOU? We were calling all over looking for you. Where were you?"

As soon as he saw his mother's face, Zach knew he was in big trouble. "I was cutting across Old Man Klapper's yard and he shot me in the back. . . . Want to see?" he blurted. He turned around and lifted up his shirt in a bid for his mother's sympathy.

It worked. Zach's mom took one look at his back and forgot that she was mad at him. "Mike!" she called to her husband. "Look at this! I never heard of such a thing. Shooting a child just for trespassing. I'll call the doctor."

"Don't call the doctor, Barbara," Zach's dad said. "It's only rock salt. All he has to do is take a bath. But I think that I'll have a word with Mr. Klapper after we finish dinner."

"That man ought to be arrested," Zach's mom said. "It's all red, honey. Does it hurt?"

"The boy was trespassing, Barb. Klapper was within his rights," Zach's dad said, watching her lead Zach down the hall toward the bathroom. "Don't scrub. You'll just make it worse," he called after them. "Soak."

By the time Zach had finished soaking the salt off his back, the rest of family was almost finished with dinner. His mother put some pasta with chicken and mushrooms on his plate. Normally, Zach spent several minutes picking the mushrooms out of his food and lining them up on the edge of his plate, where they remained until they were scraped into the garbage. But tonight he was so hungry he forgot to pick them out.

Zach looked up from his plate and met his mother's eyes. "You ate your mushrooms and they didn't kill you," she said, smiling.

"I did?" he asked.

His mom nodded. "You did."

"I guess I was hungry. We had to wait a long time for Mr. Klapper to go inside so we could sneak back across his yard after he shot me. There's no other way in or out of the canyon since they put up that fence."

"Mr. Matsuda was talking about it after karate," Lucy said. "He can't believe that the people in this town are just letting it happen."

Zach's mom sighed. "Everybody is waiting for somebody else to save the canyon. I'm afraid that it's too late now. But I have half a mind to start a petition to recall the members of our city council who voted for the development."

"That's it!" Zach said. His family turned to stare at him.

Zach nodded and took a sip of water while everybody watched. He swallowed and said, "I'm starting a petition. I'm going to get all the kids I know to pass it around. Everybody will sign it."

"Good idea," Dad said. "You can take it to school."

"D-a-a-d," Lucy said in that how-dumb-can-you-be way of hers, "We can't pass petitions around school. You have to have the principal's permission."

"Besides, it's not going to be just for kids. It's got to be for everybody who lives in this town," Zach said. "Nobody would pay attention if just kids signed it."

"Why not? Kids are important," Ben said.

"They just won't," Zach said.

Mom stood up and began clearing the table. "I know you want to do something to save the canyon, Zach, but I don't want you going door-to-door."

"But, Mom," Ben protested, "he has to. Otherwise how is he going to get people to sign a petition? I'll go with him."

Mom took Ben's plate. "No. It's dangerous. A boy in New Jersey was murdered last year going door-to-door selling candy for his school."

"Mom, what you're saying is that we can't do it," said Zach.

"No, I'm not saying that at all. You could have a meeting and pass a petition around for everybody to sign. The community room at the library may be free. I'll look into it for you kids."

She's just trying to make up for saying we can't take a petition door-to-door, Zach thought, taking a sip of water. The library will never let us use their community room. Zach picked up his plate and carried it to the sink where Ben was loading the dishwasher.

"How's your back feeling?" his father asked him.

"It still stings."

Zach's dad picked up the telephone. "I'm calling Klapper."

"Don't, Dad," Zach said, but it was too late.

"Hello, Mr. Klapper. This is Mike Barnes, your neighbor down the street. That was my son you shot this afternoon." There was a moment of silence, and then Zach's dad's voice rose. "Wait a minute, Mr. Klapper. You listen to me! I know he was trespassing. But all you had to do was ask him to leave." There was another silence, and then Zach's father turned to look at Zach. "A pickax?" he said. "Let me get this straight. Are you telling me that you shot my son with rock salt because he was about to take a pickax to your orange tree?"

"It's not true," Zach cried. "I wasn't going to hurt his tree."

His father said, "Thank you, Mr. Klapper," and hung up the phone. He glared at Zach and demanded, "What were you doing in Mr. Klapper's backyard with a pickax and a shovel?"

Zach looked down at his feet. "We were digging with them."

"You were digging in Mr. Klapper's backyard?"

"No, Trevor and I were trying to dig a trap in the canyon."

His dad got this funny look on his face. "What were you going to trap?"

"A bobcat," Zach lied. "I wanted a picture of one for a junior wildlife photography contest I saw in a magazine."

"A bobcat?" Dad said, his voice full of scorn. "I don't believe you."

"We couldn't dig one anyway. The ground was too hard," Zach said lamely.

"That's just as well," his dad said. "No more cutting through Mr. Klapper's property without his permission. Do you understand that?"

Zach nodded his head. "Are you going to call him back?"

"I'll tell him you weren't trying to chop down his tree and apologize for you this time because it's Mr. Klapper. Don't let there be a next time. The neuroscience meetings are in Washingon next week, and I don't want to hear about you giving your mother any grief while I'm away."

His dad had called Mr. Klapper again, and Zach was just settling down to do his homework at the kitchen table when Lucy came bouncing in. "I think I might have found a place!" she said.

"What?"

"I called Mr. Matsuda at the Silver Dragon and asked if he would be willing to let us use his studio for a meeting."

"What did he say?" Zach asked hopefully. It was a perfect place. A hundred people could fit in the studio, maybe more.

"He said that he'd think about it and we should check with him tomorrow."

"He didn't say yes," Ben said, going to the refrigerator.

"But he didn't say no, either," said Lucy.

Zach was surprised. Most of the time Lucy acted as if he had cooties, which she might catch if he came too near her, but it seemed like this was different.

"Can I come, too?" Ben asked.

"Sure," Zach said, "We'll all go. It will make it harder for Mr. Matsuda to say no."

CHAPTER 7

"I'LL NEVER WORK," Trevor said. Zach had just explained his idea about the petition on their way to school. Trevor bounced a tennis ball against the sidewalk. "Bowen doesn't care what anybody thinks. All he cares about is making money." The ball slipped through Trevor's fingers and went rolling down the street. He ran after it, scooped it up, and was back beside Zach in a matter of seconds.

"First you tell me that I don't have any ideas, then when I have one, you say it won't work. Do you have a better one?" Zach demanded angrily.

Trevor turned to stare at Zach in openmouthed amazement.

"Digging booby traps?" Zach asked scornfully. "Wrecking trucks?"

"Yeh," Trevor answered with a sharp nod of the head. "Sabotaging them every step of the way. That'll stop them."

"No, it won't. It will just get us into trouble."

Trevor tossed the ball in the air. "Nobody made you pull up those stakes, Zach. You were hot to do it."

45

"Maybe, but not anymore," said Zach.

Trevor caught the ball and bounced it hard against the pavement. "Suit yourself," he said.

Lucy, Zach, and Ben met in front of Canyon Vista School at three o'clock to walk to Mr. Matsuda's studio. "We have to plan out what we're going to say to him," Lucy said, taking charge. Zach and Ben looked at each other knowingly. That was their big sister Lucy!

"Why do we have to plan anything, Lucy? I thought we were asking him to let us use his studio for our meeting," said Zach.

"Duh!" Lucy replied. "We have to present the idea the right way. And we can't all talk at once. One person should do the talking." It was obvious that Lucy thought she should be that person.

A kickboxing class had just ended when they arrived at the Silver Dragon. Mr. Matsuda was wiping the sweat from his face. He put the towel down and greeted Lucy with a broad smile. "Lucy! How are you? And these must be your brothers. We have to get them in a class, too."

Lucy put her hands together and bowed to her teacher. "I keep trying, Sensai. But we are here to see if you have thought about my request."

"I have, Lucy, and I'm afraid I have to say no. This is my place of business. I earn my living here. I can't afford to cancel any classes."

"There are no classes on Sunday," Lucy pointed out quickly.

Mr. Matsuda shook his head. "I can't be here then. I think you are doing a good thing. But if there was any damage, I don't know if my insurance would cover it. You get a bunch of kids together, they can do a lot of damage."

"They wouldn't do that," Lucy insisted.

"How can you be sure?" he asked quietly.

Lucy didn't answer, and the conversation about the studio seemed to be over except for polite wishes of good luck. Zach couldn't let that happen. "Mr. Matsuda!" he said. "What if we promise to clean the place after the meeting and put every-thing back like it was before? I know you want to save the canyon. Please let us use the studio. We will ask our parents to chaperon our meeting if you want. It'll just be for a couple of hours."

Mr. Matsuda hesitated for a half a second. Seeing an open-ing, Lucy looked up at her teacher with a dazzling smile. "Ple-e-ease," she begged. "We'll prove that we are respon-sible. We'll come in and help after school. We'll answer phones, mop the floor, take out the trash—we'll do anything you want us to do."

Mr. Matsuda thought for a moment and sighed. "Okay. But I can't let you in here without a letter from your parents that says they will take responsibility for any damages. If they agree, and you show me that you can be trusted, then okay, you can have your meeting next Sunday."

"Thank you, Sensai. You won't be sorry," Lucy promised.

"I hope not," he said, as they were leaving the studio. "And don't forget to bring the letter from your parents. They need to be here to supervise the meeting. No parents, no deal."

Lucy made up a work schedule as soon as they got home from the Silver Dragon. Zach, who always complained when it was his turn to clean the room he shared with Ben, didn't say a word when Lucy told him that he would have to mop the studio floor on Wednesday and clean the bathroom on Friday.

That evening Lucy asked her mom to write the letter to Mr. Matsuda.

"What you are asking me to do is not trivial. I have to talk to Dad about it," their mom said.

Tears sprang to Lucy's eyes. "Why do you have to talk to Dad? I thought you were all for us saving the canyon?"

"I am, darling. But you have to understand what you are asking. We would be legally liable for this. If anything gets broken, we'll have to pay for it. I can't agree to something like that without talking to Dad," she explained.

"But Mom, you know he's going to say yes. And we don't have a lot of time," Lucy pleaded.

"Dad will be back from Washington tomorrow evening and we can talk about it then," Mom said, putting an end to the discussion.

The Barnes children went back to the Silver Dragon without the letter the following day. "Our dad is away on business, and our mom won't sign anything without him," Lucy explained.

"I tell you what," said Mr. Matsuda, "why don't you move your meeting back a week? It will give you more time to get the word out. And you can have more time to practice cleaning up."

Great, thought Zach.

Lucy barely let her father put down his briefcase that evening. "Dad, you have to write to Mr. Matsuda or he won't let us use the Silver Dragon to save the canyon," she blurted out.

"Write what?"

"A letter saying you will be responsible for any damage to his studio," Ben explained.

"Good going, Ben!" said Zach. "Now he'll never do it."

"Yes, I will. Your mom called me last night, and we decided we would sponsor your meeting. We are taking a chance because we trust you and we are proud of what you are doing. But if anything happens it could cost our family a lot. Now can I put my things down and go wash up? I'm beat."

Zach felt uncomfortable. He understood that his parents thought it was a big thing to write that letter, but he didn't think that it was as big a deal as they were making it out to be. Nobody was going to do anything stupid, he'd make sure of it.

Suddenly Zach realized that the date for the meeting was only eight days away and they hadn't told anybody! They had to get moving. After dinner, Zach and Ben made up a flyer on the computer announcing the meeting. It said,

49

CALLING ALL KIDS! CALLING ALL KIDS!
SAVE SAN RAMON CANYON
Find out how you can stop the bulldozers
4 p.m. Sunday, October 15
Silver Dragon Martial Arts Studio
3275 San Ramon Blvd.

Lucy and Zach took the flyer to the copy shop after school the next afternoon. When they tried to pay for the copies, the clerk wouldn't take their money. "I go running down there and I'm all for anything that will stop them from developing it," he said.

The copy shop clerk's generosity made Zach smile. Everybody must feel the same way he did about the canyon! The next afternoon, a teenage boy stopped Zach as he was stapling a flyer to a telephone pole. He asked for a bunch of flyers to hand out to his friends. Zach felt positively stratospheric! He had visions of hundreds—maybe thousands—of people parading down San Ramon Boulevard to deliver their petition to the San Ramon City Hall, led by him, Zachary Barnes!

But on Saturday, when he was standing in front of the market handing out flyers, a man wearing red-checkered golf pants told him, "You don't have any business doing this. San Ramon Canyon belongs to the Bowen Corporation." Other people hurried by as if he wasn't there. Still others took his flyers and dropped them on the ground without even looking at them.

A humongous puffy-faced woman wearing flip-flop sandals, a long flowing dress, and dangling earrings took a flyer from Zach and walked away to read it. She came back a minute later. "Your parents put you up to this," she said accusingly.

Zach was taken aback by her anger. "No, they didn't," he said.

"How old are you?"

"Eleven and a half."

"Shame on them for using their children to fight their political battles. Who are your parents?"

"Mike and Barbara Barnes," Zach said, "and they didn't put me up to anything. This is my idea. You can call them yourself and ask." He hoped she wouldn't, though.

As he watched the woman walk to her car, Zach saw Trevor across the parking lot. He called his name, but Trevor disappeared inside the market without acknowledging him. Zach was sure Trevor had seen him. Something was the matter. All of a sudden, Zach didn't feel like handing out flyers anymore. He went into the store and walked up and down the aisles until he found Trevor in the snack section. "Hey Trev, what's going on? Didn't you see me? I waved to you."

"No," Trevor replied.

"I was passing out flyers."

Trevor held up two packages of chips. "Which do you think I should get, Zach? Ranch or nacho?"

"I don't know. Whatever," said Zach.

"The nachos, I think. Hey, seeing you reminds me—Brian and I met this kid at the baseball card store this afternoon who collects rookie cards. He has some doubles that he wants to trade. We told him about you and he said you should give him a call."

"I didn't know you were going to Wigley's," Zach said, feeling left out.

"I called but you weren't home."

"I told you we were going to be handing out flyers for the meeting today."

"Here, let me give you the guy's number," Trevor said. He fished a crumpled piece of paper out of his pocket and handed it to Zach.

"I probably don't have any cards he wants," Zach said. "Hey, do you want to help me hand these out?"

Trevor shook his head. "Brian's coming over and we're watching the game." He grabbed a bag of chips and a can of salsa and headed to the express checkout line.

Zach followed him. "Are you coming to the meeting?"

"Sure," said Trevor. "But I don't think a bunch of people signing a petition is going to save the canyon. Action, hitting him where it hurts, that's all Bowen understands. When you are ready to do something that matters, let me know." He paid the checkout clerk and walked out the door. "See you," he said.

Zach watched Trevor disappear among the cars. For a second he considered running after him and spending the rest of the day laughing and watching the game with his friends. Then he turned and went back to handing out flyers.

CHAPTER 8

B Y THE FOLLOWING Saturday morning the Barnes kids had papered the town of San Ramon with "Save the Canyon" posters. Tomorrow was the big day and Lucy had called a council of war in the kitchen after breakfast to plan it. Bossy as ever, she started by handing out assignments. "Zach, you, Ben, and Dad are going to be in charge of seating," she told them. "Dad is going to bring the chairs over from church. You two will unload the van and set them up. After the meeting you take them down again and load them back into the van."

For the first time in his life, Zach was grateful to Lucy for taking over. He hadn't even thought about chairs. Lucy had thought of everything. She had even enlarged some of the photographs he had taken in the canyon to decorate the room during the presentation.

"Dad has a big aerial map of the canyon. Ask him if we can have it, Ben, will you? I talked to Mrs. Biggs at the public library and she is finding me an old map of San Ramon when it was the Black Star Ranch. Isn't that cool?" she asked.

Lucy didn't wait for an answer but went right to the next thing on her list. "Ben, did you put in all of the changes in the petition? Good. Then print out a clean copy and take it to the copy shop."

"How are we going to pay for it?" Ben asked.

"I thought we agreed that we were all going to put in some of our birthday money," Lucy said.

Even though Lucy had told him several times that he should write out his speech, Zach hadn't really thought about what he was going to say until he and Ben were setting up the chairs at the Silver Dragon. There were one hundred chairs and each of those chairs would hold a person who would be looking at him, waiting for him to say something.

Fifteen minutes before the meeting was scheduled to begin there was nobody there except for the three of them. Even their dad and mom had gone out to get coffee. Zach went to look out at the parking lot. It was empty except for a woman walking a white poodle.

"What if nobody comes?" he asked Lucy. She was pinning his photographs of the canyon to the bulletin board she had set up near the entrance to the studio.

"Don't worry," she said. "Will you hand me those tacks?"

Ten to four. Still nobody there except Mom and Dad, who were sipping their coffee in the front row. Where were Robert and Brian? Zach wondered. They said they would come. Maybe he should call them. He was just about to go to the telephone when a dark-haired woman came in and sat in a chair near the back of the room. She looked familiar. "Who is she?" Zach whispered to Ben.

"She looks like that reporter on the channel 8 news," Ben whispered back.

"What's she doing here?"

Ben shrugged. "Beats me."

Zach couldn't believe it. Channel 8 news was covering their meeting? Though anyone could come, he had been thinking of it as a kids' meeting. But maybe it was turning into something more—something bigger than he had imagined. Zach's stomach contracted in fear. Now was definitely not the time to throw up, he thought.

Kids started to trickle in, one or two at a time at first. The next thing Zach knew, every chair in the room was filled and kids were sitting and standing along the walls. "I don't know what to say," he said to Lucy.

"Haven't you written your speech?" Lucy asked in a fierce whisper. "Zach, I can't believe you," she began, then stopped. "Hey, isn't that Old Man Klapper?"

Oh no, Zach thought miserably. Now he definitely was going to throw up. He wished the floor would open and swallow him. It was a minute before four and he had absolutely no idea what to tell these people. Why should they listen to him anyway?

Zach looked at the crowd. Kids were talking to one another across the room the way they do in school assemblies. He saw his friends Brian and Robert waving to him from the side of the room, and his teacher, Ms. Mason, but he didn't see Trevor. He did see Jacob Lindstrom, another boy from his class, who gave him the thumbs-up sign.

Suddenly, as if by an invisible signal, the room became quiet. A hundred pairs of eyes focused on Zach. He looked back at the sea of faces and his knees wobbled. His heart was pounding and his mouth was dry. He opened his mouth to speak and no sound came out. He tried again. "Hi, everybody" he said, and the room roared back, "Hi!"

"I'm Zach Barnes," he said, surprised at the sound of his own voice. "We're all here because we want to save the canyon from development. We have a plan, but we need your help to carry it out." He paused for a second to see if the audience was with him. He saw his mom nodding her head encouragingly at him over her coffee cup, and continued, feeling a little less shaky. "Our plan is to circulate a petition to make the city council stop the development of San Ramon Canyon before it's too late. We want them to turn the canyon into a public park, like they said they would. We need your help getting people to sign the petition. There are copies on your chairs."

"You spelled *council* wrong, Zach," called a voice from the first row, followed by a short burst of laughter.

"Thanks, Ms. Mason. We'll fix that. But first Lucy wants to tell you a little bit of the history of San Ramon Canyon and the Bowen Corporation. Lucy?" Zach said, and moved to take Lucy's seat.

Lucy hurried to the front of the room, clutching her speech. She smiled at the crowd and suddenly her face froze. Zach realized she was even more frightened than he was. Lucy looked down at her speech and started to read in a soft, hurried voice. The audience started to whisper to one another. "Louder!" somebody yelled.

Lucy stared out at the audience, her eyes large with terror. A calm man's voice called out, "Don't read. Just talk to us." It was Old Man Klapper.

Lucy blinked stupidly as if she hadn't heard until an older girl in the front row repeated "Talk to us" in a loud whisper. Then Lucy lowered the piece of paper to her side and took a deep breath. "Okay," she said. "Can you hear me?"

The audience shouted, "Yes," and she started again. "I did some research in the library and I found out that Mr. Raymond Bowen bought the Black Star Ranch in 1952 for eighty-five thousand dollars. Since then Mr. Bowen and his corporation have built hundreds of houses on the land and made millions and millions of dollars selling them. In 1999, the city council discussed buying the canyon from him and turning it into a public park. Mr. Bowen's son-in-law, Jim Fletcher, is on the city planning commission and his nephew Tom Bowen is a city councilman and they helped vote the project down. Mr. Bowen wants to build another housing development in the canyon. There isn't one park in this city for all the people he's sold houses to. Parks don't make money. Houses do. What we have to tell Mr. Bowen is:

Enough houses! We need a park."

Above the clapping, they heard Old Man Klapper shout, "That-a-girl, Lucy!"

Lucy flushed and scurried back to her seat in the front row.

Zach stood up to take over from Lucy. "Are there any questions?" he asked.

A boy who was slouched in his chair with his legs stuck out into the aisle grumbled loud enough for everyone to hear, "Yeh. Can't Bowen do what he wants with it? It is his property."

Zach swallowed hard and glared at the boy. "He owns the canyon, but Bowen and his corporation don't own me, or you. He may have built our houses, but our families bought them and we live in them. This is our town. We have a right to tell him and the city council that we don't like his plans."

"The city council doesn't care what we think," the kid grumbled to the other boys sitting near him.

Zach was surprised by the negative response and fought to recover his train of thought. "How many of you used to go down to the canyon before they closed it off?" he asked.

Everybody raised their hands.

"What did you do there?" he asked.

"Play around with my friends," an eight-year-old girl answered.

"Explore," a boy shouted from the back of the room.

"Ride my mountain bike," another boy said.

"Chill out. Smoke. Drink beer," a big kid sitting in the

back of the room said loud enough for everyone to hear.

The boy sitting beside him laughed.

"And don't forget making out with girls," he added.

A teenage girl turned in her seat to face them. "Cut it out, you guys!"

The boy who had started it all turned to his friend and smirked. The other boy jerked his head at the door and the two of them stood up to go. There was a stir as they left the room. Zach was afraid that other kids would leave too, but no one else did.

"I guess they don't want to help save the canyon," Zach said after they left. "But the rest of you might. Where will you go to play and explore? You can't go to the canyon anymore. The Bowen Corporation has put up a fence with NO TRESPASS-ING signs. How many of you want to help us circulate this petition asking the city council to turn the canyon into a park?"

"Shouldn't we discuss the petition first?" a boy standing on the side asked.

"Yes," Zach agreed. "Anybody feel that there is something we need to add?"

Lucy took out a pen and a copy of the petition to make notes.

"Aside from a few grammatical and spelling errors, it seems fine to me. Good luck!" said Ms. Mason. She passed her marked copy to Lucy among murmurs of agreement.

"I think we should take a vote on it," said an older girl from Lucy's school.

"Okay," said Zach. "How many are for the petition?"

Everyone in the room put up their hand, even Mr. Klapper.

"I guess it's unanimous," Zach concluded. "We'll have copies of the revised petition ready for you to circulate tomorrow. You can pick them up at our house at 623 Canyon Road after school. We'll have a box of them out on the front porch in case no one's home."

A red-haired girl turned to the girl sitting next to her and whispered something in her ear. The second girl put her hand up. "My friend and I want to know, are we supposed to take the petition door-to-door?"

Lucy stood up and walked to the front of the room. She seemed like her old self again. "You can if you want to—and if it's okay with your parents—but we should be able to get enough signatures if you ask everybody you know to sign it. Are there any other suggestions?"

"What about having a car wash to raise money to pay for stuff like copying the petition?" a boy called out. Zach was surprised to see that it was Robert.

"Great idea," Lucy agreed. "Can you organize one?"

"We could have an old toy and game sale," a girl suggested.

"And a bake sale in front of the market on Saturday," said another girl.

"We should write letters to the city council telling them how we feel," an older boy sitting in the back of the room said.

"They won't pay any attention," another boy retorted.

Old Man Klapper stood up. Zach held his breath, afraid of what he might say. "Thank you for letting me attend your meeting. I know I am overage," Mr. Klapper began, and a couple of kids laughed. "As some of you know, I live on the bluffs overlooking the canyon." He looked directly at Zach, whose face grew warm. "The Bowen Corporation has closed the trail into the canyon and some of you have tried to cut across my property to get down there, which is one of the reasons I came this afternoon. I like my privacy and I don't like having my backyard trampled and my dog provoked."

Zach was astounded. Rogue provoked? Rogue didn't need to be provoked. He'd just as soon take a bite out of someone as wag his tail.

Mr. Klapper continued, "But that is not all I'm unhappy about. I don't like the Bowen Corporation's plans to develop the canyon. I'm glad to see somebody in this town doing something to stop them, even if it is a group of kids. The Gospel says, 'And a little child shall lead them.' I'll take twenty of your petitions, and I don't think I'll have a problem getting enough signatures to fill them all.

"Someone said something about writing letters. I can tell you from experience this is a great idea. Write letters to the city council, to Mr. Bowen, and to whomever else you can think of. And if you send copies of your letters to the newspaper, *The Blade* will print them. They're always desperate for news."

"We need a name for our campaign," Brian said. "I say we call ourselves Kids for Saving San Ramon Canyon."

"The Kids' Campaign to Save San Ramon Canyon," Ms. Mason corrected him.

"That's too long," a boy called out.

"Save San Ramon Canyon, then," another boy shouted. There was a chorus of yeses from the audience. Zach called for a vote and it passed by a wide margin.

Lucy passed a clipboard around for everyone to sign their names and put down their addresses, telephone numbers, and how many petitions they thought they would need. Then the meeting ended, but twelve kids stayed after the meeting to help clean up and fold chairs.

Zach and Lucy were stacking the folded chairs near the door when Judy Estrada, the channel 8 reporter, came over to talk to them. "It was a good meeting. Was it your idea to start a petition?" she asked them.

Zach glanced at Lucy. For once she wasn't taking over. "Actually, my mom said something that gave me the idea. Lucy here was our main planner. Ben, over there, did the stuff on the computer. And we all wrote the petition."

Judy Estrada flashed a dazzling smile. "I saw one of your flyers and I thought it might make a good story, but I need more to convince my producers. Here's my card. Let me know when you're ready to give your petition to the city council. Maybe I can have a camera crew there." Zach stared after her as she walked to the door.

"Dad, Dad!" Ben yelled excitedly. "Did you see? Judy Estrada from channel 8 news came to our meeting."

"Mom and I saw her," their dad said. "You guys did great."

"Judy said so, too," Ben continued, "but it isn't going to be on the news yet."

"She has to wait for us to give the city council the petition," Lucy explained.

Zach's eyes were shining with excitement as he helped his father carry the chairs to their SUV. "Can you believe how many people came?" he said. "Over a hundred. And they all voted for our petition. Lucy says we're going to have to get over a thousand printed."

"Looks like you've started a movement, Zach," Dad said.

CHAPTER 9

ZACH COULDN'T SLEEP. He kept going over the meeting in his mind. When he told the guys in the back of the room that Bowen might own the canyon, but he didn't own him, that was good. But asking what they did in the canyon was bad. Trevor is going to say something about that. Zach could hardly wait to tell him about it.

Why hadn't Trevor been there, anyway? Brian was there. So was Robert. Trevor knew about the meeting; he'd promised he'd be there. Some best friend he was!

The next morning Zach was still stewing about it. He sat on the front steps waiting for Trevor and thinking how he was going to tell him off. He should have been there even if he thought it was a waste of time. Friends support each other. But then, he wasn't exactly supporting Trevor, either. Maybe he should just forget about it.

Zach looked up and spotted Trevor coming down the street. He got up and fell into step beside him as he passed the house. They walked in silence a way. Then Trevor said, "I saw the kid I told you about who collects rookie cards. He said you didn't call. It makes me look bad, Zach. I said you would. I told him you have Shawn Green's rookie card and Sammy Sosa's, and the kid really wants them in case the Dodgers win the series."

Zach didn't respond.

"Did you see the catch Griffey made in center field yesterday? That will put him in the Hall of Fame for sure. It was even better than that famous catch by Willie Mays—the one you see on television all the time where he turns his back to home plate and runs straight back and still catches the ball. Griffey jumped clear above the wall, caught the ball, and never looked back. Man, it was like the guy had radar in the back of his head!"

"You watched the game yesterday? I can't believe it, Trevor," Zach said, without bothering to hide his irritation.

Trevor looked at him openmouthed. "What? Oh, I forgot. You had your meeting yesterday. How'd it go?"

Zach didn't answer. As soon as they reached the schoolyard, he walked away, leaving Trevor behind. He couldn't remember feeling this mad at his friend. Zach managed to stay away from Trevor for the rest of the day, but there was no avoiding him on the way home from school.

"Want to go to Wigley's?" Trevor asked as they started up the hill.

Zach shook his head. "I have to do something," he said coolly.

"What's more important than going to Wigley's?" Trevor demanded.

Zach sighed wearily. "Not that you care, but I have to go home to hand out copies of the Save San Ramon Canyon petition."

"Can't it wait?" Trevor asked.

Zach shook his head.

"I hear they got in a new shipment of baseball cards," Trevor said.

"I can't," Zach said with a shrug. He hesitated, knowing before he asked what Trevor's answer would be, then added, "You can help me hand them out and then we can go."

"No thanks," Trevor said, and walked off.

The signed petitions started arriving at the Barnes house only three days later. Lucy, Ben, and Zach were in the kitchen counting signatures when the telephone rang. Zach hurried to pick up the phone before it disturbed their mother. She was giving a piano lesson and hated it when her students had to compete with a ringing telephone. A man asked to speak to Zachary or Lucy Barnes.

"I'm Zachary," Zach said, thinking it must be a mistake because nobody besides Trevor and Brian ever called him. "Who is this?"

The man said that he was Charles Klapper Jr., and Zach's heart jumped. "You know my father. He lives a few doors away," the man continued. "I'm calling about a photograph of

67

a mouse my father saw at a meeting the other day. I was very excited when he described it to me, and he thought you could tell me where it came from."

"I took that picture," Zach said. "What do you want to know about it?"

"Do you remember where you took it? It might be important."

Zach said he had taken the picture in San Ramon Canyon. "Unbelievable," Mr. Klapper's son said. "That's great news! Are you sure?"

"Of course I'm sure," Zach replied. Who was this guy? he wondered. He sounded weird.

"Wonderful! Would it be possible for me to see the picture?" Mr. Klapper asked.

"You'll have to talk to my mother. She's busy right now. Bye," he said, and hung up the phone. Weird, positively weird, he thought.

Zach forgot about Charles Klapper Jr. until the next afternoon. The phone rang as his mother was showing one of her piano students out, and she answered it. "Yes, Zachary took those pictures for a photography contest," she said. There was a long pause. "I see. This afternoon would be as good a time as any, Mr. Klapper. Good-bye," she said. She hung up the phone, then turned and looked at Zach. "Why didn't you didn't tell me Mr. Klapper's son was interested in your photographs, Zach?"

"Mom, the guy was weird," Zach said. "He got all excited

about a picture of a mouse!"

"He's a biologist from the U.S. Fish and Wildlife Service, so it's not weird at all. I don't know why he wants to see your picture, but we'll ask him when he comes."

Charles Klapper Jr. showed up at the Barneses' front door ten minutes later. Zach was surprised at how little he looked like his father. Except for a fringe of white hair, Old Man Klapper was bald. He had fierce dark eyes and bushy black eyebrows and sagging cheeks that quivered when he spoke. His son had a wispy carrot-colored beard and wispy carrot-colored hair on his head and arms. He had carrot-colored freckles all over and golden-brown eyes that seemed huge behind his thick glasses.

Zach's mother led him into the kitchen and sat him down with a cup of coffee and Zach's photograph of the mouse. The biologist looked at the picture of the mouse for several minutes. Then he took off his glasses and looked at it again. When he was through examining the photograph, he pulled out a map of the canyon and asked Zach to show him where he had found the mouse. Zach said he couldn't tell on the map.

Mr. Klapper smiled and said, "Could you take me there?"

"Sure," said Zach. "I guess your dad doesn't mind you cutting through his backyard?"

"No, he'd let me through, I think, but we'd better make this visit official. We're going to ask them to unlock the gate for us."

Charles Klapper made a call on his cell phone. He

stopped at his car to get a couple of traps and then he and Zach walked to the entrance of the canyon. It couldn't have taken them more than fifteen minutes, but a man in a Bowen Corporation truck was waiting for them. "Are you Klapper? How long do you think you'll be?" he asked, unlocking the gate for them to go through.

Charles Klapper looked at Zach. "How long do you think it will take to find the place?"

Zach shrugged his shoulders. "I don't know."

"I'll be waiting here for you," the man said. "Try to make it quick."

Zach led the biologist down the trail to the bottom of the canyon where he remembered taking the pictures, but the mouse hole wasn't there. "It has to be near here," he said, looking around. "The heron was standing right there." After searching for several minutes, they still hadn't found it. Zach was beginning to feel frantic. He didn't know where else to look. Why had he been so sure that he could find the place again? It was just one tiny hole and the canyon stretched for acres and acres. Feeling flustered, he suggested that they climb up the bluff a way and look around there. He led the biologist through chaparral and around clumps of cactus and over rocks until they spotted a tiny hole ringed by freshly dug sand in a bare patch of ground.

"That's it," Zach announced. Then he saw that there were several holes and he realized that he didn't know which one his mouse had popped out of or even if they were mouse holes. He turned to Charles Klapper in dismay and saw that he was smiling.

"Looks like this might be it," the biologist said. "Thanks, Zach. Do me a favor, would you tell that guy at the gate I'm going to be here awhile? You might as well go home. I'm going to see if I can trap one of these little guys and it could take a long time. They are very shy. I can't believe you got a picture of one of them."

Zach watched Charles Klapper start to lay down his traps, then he turned and headed for the gate.

"Hey, what took you so long?" called the man who was waiting for them in the truck when he saw Zach coming out of the canyon.

"I had trouble finding the place again," Zach said.

"Where's the guy from the wildlife service?"

"He wanted to poke around by himself. He said to tell you that he'll be a while," Zach replied.

The man grunted and turned up the baseball game on the radio.

Zach sat down on the curb to wait for the biologist. He wanted to find out what was so special about the mouse. But when the sun was about to set, and Charles Klapper still hadn't reappeared, Zach got up and went home.

Two weeks later, the phone rang at 6:30 in the morning just as the Barnes family was getting up. Zach's father picked up on the bedroom extension. It was Mr. Klapper. "Barnes? Take a look at today's *Blade*. There's a story that might interest you on page three," he barked, and hung up.

"Was it for me?" Lucy shouted from her room.

"No. It was Mr. Klapper," Dad shouted back. "He called to tell us to look on page three of the *Blade*."

"I'll get it," Zach volunteered. He quickly slipped on his jeans and ran down the driveway barefoot. He opened the newspaper on his way back to the house and then broke into a run, yelling down the hallway for the family to come see.

The Barneses crowded into the kitchen and huddled around the table where the newspaper lay open to page three.

POCKET MOUSE PUTS CANYON
DEVELOPMENT ON HOLD

read the headline, over a photograph of a mouse like the one Zach had taken.

> SAN RAMON, CALIF.—The U.S. Fish and Wildlife Service announced Tuesday that it has placed a small mouse on the emergency endangered species list, a move likely to delay the development of a gated community of 95 luxury homes in San Ramon Canyon.
>
> Charles P. Klapper Jr., a biologist with the service, said, "The Pacific pocket mouse is part of California's natural heritage. It is an important part of the ecology."

Klapper recognized the rare mouse in a photograph taken by 11-year-old Zachary Barnes. Ironically, the photo was spotted at a meeting organized to protest plans to develop the canyon. Klapper mounted an investigation at once.

Mr. Klapper's survey of the canyon found 39 of the rare mice concentrated in a 16-acre area of coastal sagebrush in the canyon. The mouse was once common up to two miles inland along the Southern California coast from Marina del Rey to the Mexican border. Resembling a hamster, the pocket mouse is only two inches long and believed to be the smallest member of the rodent family.

"Emergency listings such as this are necessary to protect our native species, as we attempt to restore the natural balance in this area," said Cary Detler, a spokeswoman for the U.S. Fish and Wildlife Service.

Under the listing, which took effect yesterday, the Bowen Development Corporation will not be allowed to break ground until they satisfy the U.S. Fish and Wildlife Service that development will not jeopardize the colony of endangered mice.

Zach's eyes raced down the newspaper column. His chest swelled with pride. "I'm calling Trevor," he said. The phone rang before he could pick it up.

"This is Margie Clements from channel 8 news," said a woman's voice on the other end of the phone. "May I speak to Zachary Barnes?"

"That's me," Zach replied.

"One of our reporters would like to interview you about the photo of the mouse that you took in San Ramon Canyon. Are you available this morning?"

"Sure," said Zach. Then, catching his mother's eye, he added, "but I have to go to school."

Margie Clements laughed. "What if we do it before school? And we'd like to show your picture of the mouse. We'll send a car for you in fifteen minutes. Is that too soon?"

"Ah, sure," said Zach. He hung up the phone in a daze. "I'm going to be on television," he said. "They are coming right now."

"Well if you don't want to be on television wearing nothing but your jeans and a pajama top, you had better get dressed pronto," his mother said, laughing.

Zach hurried to his room and put on his favorite T-shirt. It was black with a glowing white skull on the chest. But when he came back to the kitchen, his mother took one look at him and said, "You can't wear that. Put on something nice. I know wearing a clean shirt is against your principles, but do it just this once. For the canyon."

"This is nice. It's my nicest shirt," Zach protested.

"That may be," his mother said, "but change it anyway. Wear the maroon one."

Zach trudged back to his room and changed into the maroon shirt. He hated it, but he could tell from his mother's tone she wasn't going to give in on this.

The doorbell rang. Zach ran to answer it, but Lucy beat him there. Hearing Judy Estrada's voice through the door, Zach suddenly felt shy and went back into the kitchen.

Lucy led the reporter into the kitchen to meet the family. "You must be Mr. and Mrs. Barnes. Sorry to interrupt your breakfast. I'm Judy Estrada from channel 8 news," she said, shaking hands with them. "This emergency listing must be good news."

"It's great news," Zach's mother said. "It gives the community time to organize."

"And this must be Zachary," Judy Estrada said, extending her hand for Zach to shake. "Didn't I talk to you at that meeting?"

Zach nodded. "We're working on the petition. We have lots of signatures," he said.

"I want to be there when you present the petition to the city council." Then, turning to Zach's father and mother, the reporter said, "We're in a bit of a rush. So if you don't mind, I'm going to head out with your son now. We want to shoot the interview at the entrance to the canyon. The driver is waiting outside. We'll have him back in half an hour. Is that okay?"

The whole Barnes family followed Judy Estrada out to the waiting car and waved as they drove off. Zach wished everybody he knew could see him now sitting in back of a channel 8 news car with a reporter, but it was early and the street was deserted except for Mrs. Schneider who lived next door. She was out walking her little white dog, Bianca. Zach waved to her as the car drove by. At least she looked impressed.

They rode to the top of the street, turned the corner, and pulled to a stop in front of the fence blocking off the canyon. The camera was already set up. There were big shiny panels positioned by the gate. Judy Estrada spent a minute going over some notes with Zach, and showed him where she wanted him to stand and how to speak into her microphone. Then she positioned herself and Zach in front of the camera with the NO TRESPASSING sign right above their heads. She smiled reassuringly at Zach, then the cameraman signaled and her expression became solemn. "The fight to stop the development of this canyon," she began, "took on a new life today with the discovery that it is home to a colony of rare Pacific pocket mice. The mice, which were once common, are now almost extinct, but a colony of thirty-nine of them was discovered by Zachary Barnes here."

Judy Estrada turned to Zach with another one of her dazzling smiles. "How did you find the mice, Zachary?" she asked and held the microphone out to him.

Zachary's mouth felt dry and his voice was hoarse. "I was taking pictures of animals for a photography contest," Zach said, and held up his photograph of the mouse.

"Nice shot," said Judy Estrada. "How did you manage to

take it? I understand that the Pacific pocket mouse is shy as well as rare."

"I saw this little hole in the ground. I knew something lived down there, so I waited to see if it would come out," Zach explained, his voice sounding more natural as he went on. "I was hoping it was a snake, but it wasn't."

Judy Estrada laughed. "I bet you are glad now that it wasn't a snake."

"I sure am," said Zach. "I just thought it was a regular mouse. I didn't know it was anything special."

The cameraman circled his hand in the air and Judy Estrada said, "Thank you, Zachary. I'm sorry I can't go back with you, but we need to do an introduction to your interview. John will drive you back." Then she turned to talk with the cameraman.

Zach pictured the channel 8 news car pulling up in front of the schoolyard. He would climb out of the back like a celebrity with all the kids watching him. "Can he drop me at school?" he asked.

The man shook his head. "We told your parents we'd bring you home."

All that day, Zach thought of nothing but his interview with Judy Estrada. He told Trevor on their way to school that morning. When he reached the playground, he told Brian and Robert and Jake and some other boys in his class. During social studies he whispered the news to Melissa Fernandez, who sat next to him. She told Eliza Brydolf, who passed the news to Sara Ball. By lunchtime every kid in the sixth grade knew that Zach Barnes was going to be on the channel 8 six o'clock news.

But he didn't stop with kids. He told his teacher, Ms. Mason. He told Mr. Jones, the school janitor, Mrs. Horvath, the school librarian, and Miss Newby, the playground aide. He told the mailman, Mr. Winnick; his clarinet teacher, Mr. Katz; and Mrs. Schneider, who was out front pruning the roses in her yard when he came home from his clarinet lesson.

A few minutes before six o'clock the Barnes family—except for Zach's father, who hadn't made it home from work—gathered in the living room. Ben turned on the VCR to tape the show. "Shh! It's starting," Zach said as the news theme faded and Hap Townsend and Patti Flynn appeared on the screen.

There was a pileup of seven cars on Highway 78, a truck carrying soup cans that overturned and caused northbound traffic on Highway 5 to come to a standstill for two hours, a bank robbery in La Mesa, a drug lab discovered in Jacumba, and a boat show at the convention center. Each time a story ended, Zach thought, I'm going to be on next—but then the news anchors would begin reporting another story. He was almost ready to give up hope when Patti Flynn said, "And now here's Judy Estrada with a story about a tiny mouse that is making big trouble for the Bowen Corporation."

"Here it comes, Zach!" Ben shouted.

"Shh!" said Lucy and Mrs. Barnes.

Zach held his breath.

Judy Estrada appeared on the screen, standing in front of the fence that stretched across the top of San Ramon Canyon. She told about the pocket mouse's being put on the emergency endangered species list. That had to be the introduction Judy Estrada said she was going to tape, Zach thought. "Now, here's me," he shouted, and leaned forward expectantly. But instead of Zach, the camera cut to a tall man wearing a suit.

"Who is he?" Lucy asked.

"I don't know," Mom said. "Shh! We'll find out."

"The so-called endangered mouse was found by the same boy who organized a children's movement to protest the development," the man in the suit was saying. "And now someone has smashed one of our trucks and pulled up our surveyor's stakes, not once, but twice, costing us thousands of dollars. We have no intention of being intimidated by the actions of juvenile vandals, nor their parents who are obviously using these children. We intend to fight to protect our property and our right to develop it as we see fit. We will contest this emergency listing and we will investigate the vandalism. We have a good lead on who the perpetrators are, and when our investigation is complete, we plan to bring charges."

"That was Fred McManus of the Bowen Development

Corporation, commenting on new obstacles to the San Ramon Canyon development. Back to you, Patti."

The scene switched back to Patti Flynn and Hap Townsend at the studio. "Thanks, Judy," said Patti Flynn. "The emergency endangered species listing gives the Bowen Development Corporation and the U.S. Wildlife Service two hundred and forty days to come up with a plan that protects the Pacific pocket mouse. And now here's Andy with the sports news." Patti Flynn disappeared and a bald man wearing a tweed jacket appeared on the screen.

"Isn't Zach going to be on?" Ben asked, looking bewildered.

"No, it's over," said Lucy.

"I'm sorry, Zach," said Mom.

Zach's eyes filled. He lowered his head, trying to keep the tears back.

"Honey! Don't cry," his mother said, putting her arm around him. "They cut interviews all the time. I'm sure you were wonderful."

Zach couldn't talk. He couldn't breathe.

They knew.

CHAPTER 10

THAT EVENING ZACH couldn't eat. He managed to sit through dinner but asked to be excused from the table without touching his chocolate ice cream. He went to his room and lay on the bed, staring at the ceiling. Tomorrow, or the day after, or the day after that, they would be coming for him and Trevor.

He felt sick. He got out of bed, went to the bathroom, and sat down on the floor next to the toilet just in case he threw up. Vandalism. What did that mean? Destroying property. He bet they sent kids to one of those reform school farms for that. He would die if they sent him to one of those places. He had to warn Trevor.

Zach headed to his parents' bedroom to get the portable phone, but halfway across the hall, he heard his name and froze. "I've never known Zach to pass up dessert," his mother was saying. "That Estrada woman got him all excited about being on television and then cut the interview. It was a terrible thing to do to a kid. He told everybody he was going to be on the news. You can imagine how disappointed and embarrassed he must feel."

Zach imagined what Trevor would say when he heard about it. Suddenly he was the last person Zach wanted to speak to. He would tell Trevor tomorrow. The police wouldn't come for them at night, would they? Zach buried his face in his arms, squeezed his eyes shut, and willed himself to stop thinking, but his thoughts kept circling back on themselves like dogs chasing their own tails. It was his own fault. He knew he shouldn't have pulled up those stakes. And now he was going to go to jail for it.

He pictured his family at breakfast, his father drinking coffee and reading the newspaper, his mother standing at the kitchen counter nibbling on toast, his brother bent over a bowl of cereal, and Lucy still in the bathroom combing her hair or doing whatever she did in there. He imagined the phone ringing and his mother answering it and someone on the other end of the line saying, "This is Sergeant Wilcox, from the San Ramon sheriff's department. We are calling about your son, Zachary James. Would you mind bringing him down to the station? We want to talk to him."

He pictured himself standing before a stern-looking gray-haired judge. Trevor was beside him. The judge banged his gavel and said, "You should be ashamed . . . kids like you should know better . . . I am not going to let you off easy." He imagined his mother crying and his father putting his arm around her and leading her away, leaving him behind. Then he pictured a big, rough-looking policeman telling Trevor and him to hold their hands out to be handcuffed. In the next picture that floated through Zach's mind, he was looking at miles and miles of flat emptiness through a chain-link fence topped with razor wire. Trevor was standing behind him in an orange jumpsuit. "You should have stopped me, Zach," he said.

Zach shivered. He shook his head and bit his lip. He didn't want to go to jail.

The bathroom door rattled. "Zach, I need to get in there," Lucy shouted through the closed door.

"Go away!" he said.

"I have school tomorrow. I have to get ready for bed."

"Stop bugging me!" he yelled.

"Are you going to let me in?" She rattled the door again. There was no response. "Will you get out of there? You've been in there for hours, you little creep. Mom!" she shouted.

Zach tore off a piece of toilet paper and blew his nose. He unlocked the door and flung it open. It slammed into the wall with a bang. "Okay?" he said, glaring at his sister. He hurried past her to his room and flung himself on the bed.

He pictured all the kids at school standing in tight little groups glancing over their shoulders as he walked by. "Did you hear about Trevor and Zach?" they whispered to one another. "They wrecked that Bowen Corporation truck in the canyon and pulled up their grading stakes. And Zach thought he was so cool, starting a petition. Did you see him at that meeting, standing up there telling us how to save the canyon? He's such a fake."

Zach's chest heaved and a sob escaped. Everyone was going to hate him. He buried his head in his pillow so no one would hear him. He turned and tossed until early morning and woke up before anyone else. He couldn't put off talking to Trevor any longer. He got out of bed. He was putting his books into his book bag when his mother heard him and came into the kitchen to investigate. She looked at him closely. "How do you feel?"

"Okay," he answered.

"What are you doing up?"

"I have to talk to Trevor. It's important," he said, stuffing another book into his book bag.

"Now? It's early, Zach," she said.

"Because . . ." Zach tried to think of a reason. "Because I want to see his new baseball cards and he said if I came over this morning before school he'd show me them."

"Did you do your homework? You went to bed awfully early last night."

"Mom, I have to go."

"When is it due?"

"Not till tomorrow. I'll do it tonight. Okay?"

"Okay," she agreed, "but I don't see what could be so important this early in the morning. How's your stomach feel? Your head?"

"Fine. Fine."

"Then eat some breakfast before you go." She poured him a glass of milk and put a piece of bread in the toaster for him.

Zach gulped down the milk. He grabbed the toast in one hand and his book bag in the other, and hurried out the door.

Trevor's mother looked surprised to see Zach so early in the morning. "Trevor just woke up. He's getting dressed," she said, ushering Zach into the kitchen.

She disappeared down the hall and Zach sat down to wait. Trevor emerged a few minutes later. "Hey, what's up?" he asked.

"They know," Zach whispered looking down the hall where Trevor's mother had gone. "Come on, let's get out of here."

Trevor nodded. "Mom," he shouted down the hall. "I'm going."

As soon as they were outside, Trevor demanded, "Who knows? What?"

"Didn't you see the channel 8 news?"

Trevor shook his head.

"This man from the Bowen Corporation said they know who pulled up their stakes and smashed their truck and they're going to the police. We could end up in jail."

"My dad would never let them send me," Trevor said confidently.

"Your dad might be a good lawyer, but he can't help us if they know," Zach said.

"They don't know," Trevor said, and then gave Zach a

searching look. "Not unless you told someone. Did you?"

Zach was outraged. "No! But somebody might have seen us. I thought I saw somebody else up there when we were pulling up the stakes the first time. And remember I was wearing Lucy's purple sweat pants. You can see them a mile away."

"So? What are you telling me, Zach?"

"I don't know. Maybe if we say we're sorry. . . ."

Trevor interrupted. "No, I'm not apologizing. They're going to tear up the canyon. Let them just try to send me to jail. Let them just try!"

Zach stared at him openmouthed.

Seeing Zach's reaction, Trevor said, "Don't worry, Zach, they were probably bluffing. Those guys are liars. You can worry about it all you want, but I'm not going to. Okay?" They had reached the schoolyard now. Brian and Robert were coming toward them. Trevor stopped talking. "See you," he said and walked off to join some boys playing keep-away.

Robert and Brian stopped right in front of Zach, blocking his way. "Hey man, what happened? You said you were going to be on the news," said Robert.

Zach shrugged. "They cut my interview."

"Did you see that guy from the Bowen Corporation? Can you believe it?" Brian laughed. "He accused *us* of doing all that stuff."

Robert shook his head. "Wrecking a truck and pulling up his precious grading stakes? Would you believe it?"

Zach laughed nervously. "I know. It was pathetic."

"It's not funny, you guys," said Robert. "The guy is out to destroy our campaign."

"It's because the petition scared them. That's what my dad says. They're worried the whole town is going to come out against them," said Brian.

"Somebody should call the station and tell them the guy was lying," said Robert.

Brian shook his head. "It won't do any good."

"But we can't let him get away with saying those things. We have to do something," Robert insisted. The bell rang, and the boys headed in to class.

Zach still was thinking about what Robert had said when Ms. Mason called on him during social studies. He sputtered trying to come up with something and then had to admit that he hadn't been listening. He was still thinking about it later that day when Ms. Mason was going over some math on the board. He didn't hear her say that it was going to be on the test.

And then it came to him. On the way home from school with Trevor that afternoon, he realized what he had to do. "You know what I'm going to do, Trev?" he said. "I'm going to write a letter to the Bowen Corporation and apologize."

Trevor's eyes widened in disbelief. He stopped. "What?"

Zach continued walking, leaving Trevor standing there on the sidewalk.

"You wouldn't dare!" Trevor shouted at his back.

Zach kept on going. Trevor hurried to catch up. He grabbed Zach's arm. "Don't you dare, Zach. If you do, I'll beat you to a pulp."

Zach jerked his arm away from Trevor and walked away.

"I want to see it before you send it. I have a right," Trevor shouted at him.

"Afraid I'm going to get you in trouble?" Zach sneered at him.

"Look who's talking about being afraid," Trevor shouted, running at Zach and shoving him from behind.

Zach staggered and regained his balance. He turned around and gave Trevor a shove, saying, "Keep your hands off me!"

Trevor shoved back. "You little coward, you better show that letter to me! I don't trust you not to get us into trouble."

Zach walked away before Trevor had a chance to push him again. He didn't care what Trevor said. He had to do this. He thought about Robert and Brian and Ben and Lucy and all the other kids running around trying to get people to sign the petition. He couldn't let them down. He couldn't let the Bowen Corporation use his mistake to ruin the canyon. People wouldn't sign a petition they thought was started by a bunch of vandals. He pictured his friends' disappointed faces as the bulldozers began to roll. He'd rather go to jail than let that happen.

Zach opened the front door. One of his mother's students

was playing "Für Elyse" on the piano. He went into his room and closed the door. He sat down at the desk and opened his notebook to a blank page and wrote: *Dear Mr. Bowen.* Then he stopped, not knowing what to say next. If he just said that the kids who were passing out the petitions weren't involved, Mr. Bowen would wonder how he knew. He had to admit that he did it first and then say that nobody else was involved. Of course, he would say that he was sorry. Maybe if he explained why they pulled up the stakes, Mr. Bowen would understand. The truck was another matter. He wasn't going to say anything about that. Zach started writing, then stopped and tore the paper out of his notebook. He crumpled it into a ball and threw it in the wastepaper basket in frustration. It wasn't coming out right. He wrote a second draft, then a third. Writing was hard work, he thought. He wrote, crossed out, and started over again many times.

After a while, he heard his mother talking to her student in the hallway. The lesson must be over, which meant any minute now she was going to come looking for him. He hurriedly finished the letter, wrote *Sincerely yours* and signed his name without thinking. Then, realizing he couldn't sign his name, he crossed it out. But he couldn't leave the words *Sincerely yours* there without a name or something saying who was sincerely yours, so he wrote, *Two kids who love the canyon,* closed his notebook, and slipped it between the headboard of his bed and the wall.

On their way to school the next morning, Zach handed Trevor a folded piece of paper. "You wanted to see this before I sent it," he said.

Trevor stopped. He unfolded the paper and read:

Dear Mr. Bowen,

We are really sorry we pulled up your grading stakes. It was the wrong thing to do.

We did it to stop your company from bulldozing the canyon and building a development. We love the canyon. Everybody in San Ramon does. We want it to stay the way it is. It is a magical place.

A man from your company went on the news and told everybody that our parents put us up to it. That is a big lie. Our parents don't know what we did in the canyon and neither do the kids who are getting people to sign petitions. They didn't have anything to do with it.

Sincerely yours,
Two kids who love the canyon

"You can't send this," Trevor said as soon as he finished reading. "You're going to get us in trouble."

Zach's jaw was set. "I don't care what you say. I'm sending it, Trevor."

"Then leave me out of it," said Trevor.

"You're not in it," Zach replied.

Now Trevor was angry. "Yes, I am. You say, '*We are sorry.*' I'm not sorry. There's no way that I'm going to say I'm sorry to them. We had a good reason for doing what we did. Remember?"

Zach glared at Trevor. "That doesn't make what we did right." How could he make Trevor understand? He took a breath. "Trevor, tell me this. If what we did was okay, why don't we tell the whole world we did it?"

Trevor stared at Zach in astonishment. "Because . . . because we'd be in deep doo-doo. That's why. Sometimes you just have to do whatever it takes to stop people. Like when you're in a war and you attack the enemy before they attack you."

"But this isn't a war," Zach said.

"It *is* a war," Trevor insisted.

"It was a mistake," said Zach.

"That's what you say. I say don't send this."

"I'm going to," said Zach.

"Then you have to take out '*we*' and you can't sign it '*two boys who love the canyon*'. It's a dead giveaway," said Trevor.

Zach snorted. "What else do you want me to take out?"

"If you ask me, you can scratch the whole thing," said Trevor. "Nobody is going to pay attention to an anonymous letter anyway."

CHAPTER 11

WHEN ZACH CAME HOME that afternoon there was a note on the kitchen table saying that his mom, Lucy, and Ben had gone to the downtown library and reminding him to practice the clarinet. Zach crumpled up the note. Grabbing a glass of milk, he sat down at the computer to type the letter to Mr. Bowen. He changed all the *we's* to *I's* and the *two boys who love the canyon* to *someone who loves the canyon*. He printed it out and folded the letter, then stuffed it into an envelope. He hid it in a box of old toys in the garage where no one in the family would ever look.

He came back into the house and sat down in the kitchen to do his homework, but he couldn't concentrate. He wandered into his room, picked up his clarinet, and tried to practice the new piece Mr. Katz had assigned him to learn. After a few bars, he put it down.

Looking for something else to do, Zach took the binder with his rookie baseball cards down from the shelf. For three years he had picked out rookies that he thought were going to become great baseball players and collected their cards. If the rookies did well, the value of their cards went up. Zach had made some good choices and more than a couple of his picks had been named rookie of the year. Three of them looked as if they might become stars one day. He didn't want to sell any of those cards, but just for the fun of it he looked them up in *Beckett's Baseball Card Monthly*. He was surprised to find that one of them was worth seven dollars, another six dollars, and another fourteen dollars. Not bad, he thought, considering what he had paid for them.

That evening for the second time in his life Zach turned on the channel 8 local news at six o'clock. He sat on the edge of the couch and watched the entire program from beginning to end. There was nothing on the news about either the canyon or the vandalism. He felt like a condemned man who has been given a reprieve.

Zach went into dinner humming a song from camp. *"We will, we will rock you. We will, we will rock you."* He ate every last bite of his chicken and pasta. He even polished off some broccoli and was still hungry for dessert. He had just taken a chocolate chip cookie from the plate and was bringing it to his mouth when Lucy said, "Brittany Schindler's mother called channel 8 news to complain about that man from the Bowen Corporation who said we vandalized their building site."

"Good for her!" said Dad.

"They told her that they aren't responsible for what people say in interviews. Brittany's mother says that the Bowen Corporation always prosecutes anyone who vandalizes or steals from their building sites. I wouldn't want to be one of the kids who did it when Bowen gets a hold of them. But if they catch them at least they'll know it wasn't us."

Zach choked on his cookie. He ran to the sink. The family stopped to stare at him in alarm. His mother got up from her chair. She banged on his back, until he spit up the cookie. "It went down the wrong way," he gasped.

That night Zach couldn't sleep again. He kept hearing steel doors clanging shut in his head. Finally at 6 A.M., he got up, dressed, and slipped out of the house. It was Saturday and the neighborhood was so quiet, Zach thought he could hear the ocean three miles away. He walked up the hill to Trevor's house. He was pulling the latch on the gate to the backyard just as the sliding door to the patio opened and Purdy, Trevor's cat, sauntered out. Seeing Zach, the cat headed toward him, mewing loudly. She tangled herself in his legs and made him trip. Trying to catch his balance, Zach knocked into a wind chime hanging from a nearby eucalyptus tree and sent it clanging.

"Zach?" Trevor's dad called from the open door.

Trying to seem innocent, Zach turned and waved at Mr. Mack.

"What are you doing here so early? Trevor's still asleep. Come back later," said Mr. Mack, sliding the door shut.

Zach walked home slowly. When he got to his front door, he found he had forgotten to take a key. Perfect! He was locked out. If he rang the bell, he would wake everybody up and they would want to know what he was doing up so early. He sat down on the porch and put his head in his hands. What was he going to do? He wished that he could press the reverse button on his life like you do on the video and *presto!* the grading stakes would spring back into place with their hot pink ribbons fluttering in the breeze and the truck's tires would fill up with air and the hood would become smooth and unsmashed. But that was impossible in real life—or was it? He lifted his head and sat up straight. Money! Money was the magic reverse button! The sound of the front door opening behind him jolted him out of his thoughts. He swung his head around to see his dad standing there wearing his pajama bottoms and a puzzled expression.

"What are you doing here?" he asked.

"I locked myself out."

"At this hour?"

Zach was too tired to explain. He got up and squeezed past his dad into the house. He started back to bed but knew he'd never get back to sleep. Instead he went into the kitchen and slumped down in a chair at the table. His father came in carrying the newspaper. Zach tensed, but all his father asked him was if he wanted bacon and eggs for breakfast. Zach shook his head. "I'm not hungry."

Mr. Barnes looked at Zach with concern. "Is something

the matter, Zach? You've been acting awfully hangdog."

Zach was horrified to feel his eyes filling.

"Something is the matter," said his father. "Do you want to talk about it?"

Zach hunched over the table so his dad couldn't see his eyes. He couldn't have answered if he had wanted to.

"Okay, if that's how you feel about it, Zach. But if you change your mind, I'm here and ready to listen." His father filled the kettle with water and put it on the stove. Then he took the coffee beans and poured them into the grinder and turned it on.

"Dad," Zach said tentatively.

His father turned off the machine the instant Zach spoke. "Yes?" he said.

"Nothing," said Zach.

His father poured the ground coffee into a filter, and filled the reservoir with water. Soon the room filled with a delicious scent. The smell seemed comforting to Zach.

"Dad," he said, "what if somebody was doing something really bad and you stopped them by doing something—" he searched for the words, "something that you're not supposed to do?"

"Did you do something you weren't supposed to do?" Mr. Barnes asked.

Zach shrugged. "Just wondering."

"What made you wonder about that?"

"I don't know."

Mr. Barnes poured himself a cup of coffee and sat down across from Zach. "Well two wrongs never make a right. But I'd have to know the particulars to be able to give you an opinion."

His father's answer didn't make Zach feel any better and he fell silent. After a moment he said, "Dad, did you think the referee was right in calling a penalty the other night?" They talked about the football game and his father handed him the sports page of the newspaper. When Zach finished reading about the game, he decided he was hungry after all. He fixed himself a bowl of cereal and a piece of toast. Then he headed back to Trevor's house.

Trevor was watching television in his pajamas. "Did you fix that letter?" he asked Zach without taking his eyes from the TV.

Zach glanced at the screen, where a big caveman was clubbing a smaller caveman over the head, and then back at Trevor. "Yes," he said.

Trevor clicked the remote and the picture on the screen changed to a wrestling ring.

"I was thinking about sending some money with the letter," said Zach.

Trevor sneered at him. "You're such a coward, Zach."

Zach's face went white and then red as a tide of anger flooded through his body. "At least I'm not afraid to admit it when I do something wrong."

Trevor snorted with disgust. "Look who's talking about

being scared. You are so scared now you are practically peeing in your pants."

"Yeh right, Trevor. You act big and bad. But you are afraid to admit you could ever make a mistake. Who's sending the letter? Me, that's who."

Trevor's mouth dropped. "You didn't send it. Did you?"

"No. But only because I didn't have a stamp. It's gone as soon as I get one."

"I'll kill you if you send it, Zach. I swear I will. Now leave me alone, will you. You're making me puke," Trevor said, turning back to the television.

Zach waited a second for Trevor to laugh or say something that would show he didn't mean it. When he didn't, Zach left.

CHAPTER 12

ZACH FLEW DOWN THE stairs at Trevor's house. He rushed down the walk and turned onto the street. His mind whirled with all sorts of things he wished he'd said. So Trevor thought he could scare him? Kill him? Yeh, right. Zach would show him who was a coward. He would mail that letter as soon as he got home. Maybe he'd sign his name—no, both their names.

Zach stopped walking. What was happening to him? His best friend had just told him to leave him alone, he was making him puke. His parents were worried about him. And he could go to jail, and for what? Instead of continuing home, Zach found himself heading to the canyon. He walked up to the fence, threaded his fingers through the links and shook the fence with all of his might. "I hate this," he said, and then yelled it at the top of his lungs.

Slowly he turned and started back home. There was no way around it. He knew what he had to do. No matter what Trevor said, he couldn't let the Bowen Corporation use his dumb mistake to ruin the chance to save the canyon. If he had to, he'd confess, but maybe there was one more thing he could try first. He remembered thinking that money was the magic button that made all things possible. If he sent Bowen Corporation the money to pay for the damages he and Trevor had caused, they couldn't complain about being victims of vandalism anymore, and they'd have no reason to put him in jail.

But where was he going to get the money? He couldn't just go up to his mother and say, "Hey, Mom, I'm in trouble. Give me a hundred dollars." He couldn't work for it. It would take too long. What was he supposed to do? Rob a bank? Win the lottery? Sell something?

Sell something! That was it! He slowed down to think. His camera? No, he couldn't do that. His mom and dad would ask where it was. His bike? No, thought Zach, they'll want to know what happened to that, too. He didn't own anything worth money, unless . . . What about his baseball cards?

Zach pushed the front door open with a bang. Inside, his mother was playing a duet with her friend Julie. His father and Ben were gone, probably to Ben's violin lesson, and Lucy was talking on the telephone as usual. He hurried by without even glancing in her direction and went straight to his room. He took the binders with his baseball cards off the shelf and stuffed as many as would fit into a backpack. He slipped the pack over his arms onto his back, and put two other binders into a shopping bag and carried them out to his bike. Balancing as best he could, he wheeled his bike out of the garage, climbed on, and rode down the hill to the shopping mall on San Ramon Boulevard where Wigley's Sports Cards and Memorabilia Shop was located.

Saturday was a busy day at Wigley's. The glass cases were ringed with boys looking over baseball cards, trying to decide which ones to spend their allowance on. Zach stood aside and waited for almost an hour before Mr. Wigley noticed him. "Hey, Zach, haven't seen you for a while. I just got the new all-star cards. As soon as I take care of these other guys, I'll show them to you."

"I'm not collecting them anymore," Zach said.

"Since when? You were collecting rookies, weren't you?"

Zach shrugged. "I'm selling my cards. Do you want to buy them?"

Mr. Wigley sighed. "Have to see what you've got before I can tell you if I'm interested. But I warn you, I can only pay forty to sixty percent of what *Beckett's* says they're worth."

Even Zach, who was not an A student in math, knew that forty percent wasn't great. But it was something, and something was better than nothing. He unzipped his book bag and started to pull out the binder that contained his most valuable cards.

Mr. Wigley tried to stop him. "Zach, I don't have time for this right now. I'm real busy. Can you bring them back Monday?"

"Please, Mr. Wigley, just a quick look," he pleaded, setting the binder on the counter.

Zach had worried over the purchase of every card, changing his mind often and coming back to look at them several times before finally pulling the money out of his pocket and putting it out on the counter for Mr. Wigley. Now he watched anxiously as Mr. Wigley opened the binder and turned its pages. After a few minutes, Mr. Wigley looked up and sighed. Zach swallowed hard. "I'll give you twelve dollars for Ken Griffey Jr., eighteen dollars for Hank Aaron. I'm not interested in the rest. You might do better at a baseball card show, Zach. But I don't think you should sell them. They're more valuable as a collection."

"I need the money," Zach said. Then, realizing how this might sound, he added, "I broke a lamp in the living room and my mom is making me pay for it."

"Oh," Mr. Wigley said. "I see. Can't you find some other way to pay for it? You've spent a lot of time putting this collection together. It would be a pity to break it up."

"I'll think about it," Zach said. He thanked Mr. Wigley, and, taking the binder from the counter, put it back in the shopping bag. Weighted down with disappointment, he slumped out of the store. He climbed back onto his bike. Carrying the shopping bag full of binders while gripping the handlebars at the same time, he wheeled the bike out of the shopping center onto Canyon Road. Riding a bike up Canyon Road was slow, hard work most days, but today Zach pedaled even more slowly than usual.

What was he going to do? According to *Beckett's*, his cards were worth at least $200. It wasn't fair for Mr. Wigley not to give him what the cards were worth. He was thinking about trying his luck at another store to see if he could get a better deal when it occurred to him that he didn't have to *sell* the cards. The cards were *valuable*! If he sent the cards themselves, it would be just as good as sending money. With this thought, Zach pedaled faster until he was flying up the street.

He turned into his driveway and jumped off his bike, leaving it lying in the middle of the driveway. No one was home except for his father, who was napping. Zach went out to the garage to get his letter to the Bowen Corporation and an empty box. He brought them back to his room. Next he sat down at his desk with his baseball cards and a copy of *Beckett's Baseball Card Monthly*. He listed how much each card was worth on a sheet of paper before taking it out of the binder and putting it into the box.

Zach was still going through his baseball cards when he heard his brother come in. Ben had a way of flinging open the door that was unmistakable. Quickly, Zach hid the list and put the box under his bed before Ben reached their room.

On Sunday, the family had planned a hike in the mountains. Zach begged his mom to be allowed to stay home by himself, but she said he had to go. She didn't want him lying on the couch watching television all afternoon. After they came home, Zach managed to finish his list of baseball cards while his mom took Ben to buy shoes. He wrote a note explaining that the baseball cards were worth money and placed it in the box along with the letter apologizing to Mr. Bowen. Then he taped the box shut. He would have to wait until Monday to mail it.

On Monday morning, Zach waited for Trevor to come by so they could go to school together. Zach had decided not to talk about their fight. They had been best friends since preschool and they never stayed mad at each other for long. But Trevor didn't come. Ben and Lucy left for school and still no Trevor.

"You've got to get going," said Zach's mom. "Give him a call. Maybe he's sick."

Zach picked up the phone and called Trevor's house. Mrs. Mack told him that Trevor had left half an hour ago.

Zach put the phone down slowly. He and Trevor had always walked to school together no matter what. Sometimes after a fight, one of them would walk ahead of the other and they wouldn't exchange a word the whole way, but they still waited for each other to go to school. "He already left," he said to his mother.

"You had better get a move on, too, if you don't want to be late," said his mom.

Zach ran out the door and down the street, but his legs felt heavy. What was the point of rushing? He slowed down and walked the rest of the way with his head hunched between his shoulders. The bell had already rung by the time he reached the schoolyard, and he was marked tardy.

Zach looked back to where Trevor sat. Trevor stared straight past Zach as if he wasn't there.

At recess, Trevor and Brian went off by themselves to the edge of the playground.

Zach started to follow them, then turned away and joined some kids who were talking about a new movie that was showing at the mall.

Zach walked up the hill and home alone. All he could think about was Trevor staring through him as if he didn't exist. This wasn't the Trevor he knew, who was always ready to laugh things off. Well, thought Zach, he couldn't worry about Trevor right now. He had to get that package in the mail. He logged on to the computer and typed the address of the Bowen Corporation and printed it as a label. He grabbed the tape and scissors and was just finishing taping the label on the box of baseball cards when Ben came in. He took some money his mother had given him to buy film, and picked up the box. "I'll be right back," he called. He was out the door before Ben had a chance to respond.

Zach carried the box down Canyon Road to the post office. After he mailed the package he felt as if a load had been lifted from his shoulders.

That night Zach dreamed that he was walking up to the podium to present the petition to save San Ramon Canyon to the city council. All eyes were on him. Just as he was about to hand the petition to the mayor, a familiar figure stood up and pointed at him. It was the man from the Bowen Corporation Zach had seen on TV. "It's him!" the man cried. "He's the one who did it. Arrest him." Someone grabbed his arm. He struggled to break away.

Zach woke himself up with his thrashing. His heart was racing and his mouth was dry. It was just a dream, he told himself, just a bad dream. Tomorrow Mr. Bowen will get my baseball cards, Trevor will stop being mad at me, and it'll all be okay. Everything will be okay.

CHAPTER 13

DAYS PASSED AND still Zach was walking to school alone. He found himself avoiding looking at Trevor in class. Brian and Robert noticed that something was wrong between them, but what could Zach tell them? If he told them about the stakes and the truck, they would never speak to him again. Brian especially. He had collected more signatures for the petition than anybody else. Zach threw himself into the Save San Ramon Canyon campaign. On the weekend he and Brian set up a table at the mall and collected eighty-four more signatures for the petition. He also found himself watching the six o'clock news every night, but there were no further announcements from the Bowen Corporation. They must have gotten my baseball cards and decided not to press charges after all, thought Zach. He started to relax.

He was sitting at the kitchen table counting up signatures, while Lucy looked through the newspaper for a current event for social studies. Suddenly she looked up. "Did you see this?" she asked, and slid the newspaper across the table to Zach.

DEVELOPER CRIES FOUL

Fred McManus, a spokesman for the Bowen Development Corporation, decried what he termed an absurd attempt to derail the Bowen Corporation's plans to build a housing development in San Ramon Canyon. "The opposition has stooped so low," complained McManus, "as to put their children up to trying to buy us off with baseball trading cards."

McManus said that Raymond Bowen, chief executive of the Bowen Corporation, received a box of baseball cards in the mail on Wednesday along with an anonymous letter informing him that the cards were intended as compensation for recent vandalism at the building site. According to the San Ramon police, the case is under investigation, but no charges have been filed.

"This is clearly a publicity stunt to put the Bowen Corporation on the defensive," Mr. McManus complained. "It is further harassment by environmental fanatics. Really, using children like this is despicable."

Zach's eyes raced down the page. The color drained from his face. "What's the matter, Zach?" Lucy asked. "Do you know anything about this?"

Zach acted shocked. "Me? No!"

"Are you sure?"

"Sure, I'm sure. I wouldn't give away my baseball cards." Zach slid the newspaper back across the table to Lucy and turned back to the signatures. He began counting again, but the names danced in front of his eyes and he lost count.

When Lucy left the room a few minutes later, Zach reread the story. He couldn't believe it. This Mr. McManus twisted everything! The phone interrupted him. He didn't want to answer it, but his mom would be ticked off if it disturbed the piano lesson she was giving in the other room.

"Barnes residence," he said.

"Hello, this is Judy Estrada from channel 8 news. May I speak to Zachary Barnes, please?"

Zach caught his breath. "Yes?" he answered cautiously.

"Zach? Hi, sorry that we couldn't use your interview. It was a heavy news day."

"Uh-huh," Zach said.

"Do you know anything about that box of baseball cards that was sent to Mr. Bowen?" Judy Estrada asked.

"What baseball cards?" Zach asked.

She sounded disappointed. "Oh, I thought if anybody would know about it, you would. My sources say it was sent by the Save San Ramon Canyon group."

"They didn't have anything to do with it," Zach replied angrily.

"Do you know that for a fact?" she probed.

109

"Yes."

"Will you tell me how you know?" she asked.

"I can't," he said.

"The Bowen Corporation is saying that the cards were sent as a publicity stunt."

"I didn't . . ." He stopped, horrified at his slip.

"You didn't what?"

Zach didn't answer.

"Send them? You did send them, didn't you, Zach?" said Judy Estrada.

Zach felt trapped. The *I* hung there like a pointing finger. "Yes, it was me," he said. He could imagine what Trevor would do if he told the reporter about him. He would never talk to him again. "I pulled up the stakes. Nobody put me up to it. I was just mad."

"I understand, Zach, but why did you send those baseball cards?"

"They're worth money. Some cards are worth lots of money. One was auctioned off for more than half a million. I read about it in the paper. I didn't have any money, but I had baseball cards," Zach went on. "I love them. I've been collecting them a long time. But I would rather have the canyon any day. I wish I had enough cards so I could buy the whole place, because it really should be a park."

While Zach was talking, Lucy came into the kitchen. She stood in the doorway listening quietly until Zach hung up the phone. "Liar," she said. "You told me you didn't know anything about it. *'I wouldn't give away my baseball cards,'*" she mimicked. "Mom!" she yelled.

Their mother rushed into the kitchen. "Are you two fighting again?"

Zach blurted, "I sent Mr. Bowen my baseball cards," before Lucy could tell on him.

"Tell her about the vandalism, Zach," said Lucy.

"What's this about?" Mrs. Barnes asked.

Before Zach had a chance to answer, the front door opened and their father called, "Hi honey, I'm home!" He walked into the kitchen with a smile on his face. He took one look at them standing there, and his face fell. "What's going on?" he asked.

"I'm waiting for Zach to tell me," Mrs. Barnes said.

Zach gulped. He looked from his mother to his father and then back to his mother. There was no escape. He told them the whole story—leaving Trevor's part out again. As he was coming to the end, his mother's piano student stuck her head out into the hallway and called, "Mrs. Barnes?"

"I have to go finish Amanda's lesson right now," his mother said. "But this is far from over, Zachary James."

Zach nodded miserably.

"This is serious business, Zach," said his father. "They could send you to jail if you are convicted of vandalism."

Zach nodded. He didn't trust himself to speak.

"It's not going to do you any good to cry about it now," said his dad. "You should have thought about that before. What is wrong with you? Destroying someone else's property—how could you do a thing like that?"

"We . . . I . . . just . . . wanted . . . to save the canyon," Zach said.

His father's eyes were blazing. "That is the wrong way to do it."

"They were going to bulldoze it," Zach said.

"So . . . ?" his dad demanded. "Do you think that gives you the right to destroy their property? What if everybody took the law into their own hands when someone did something they disagreed with? Think about it, Zach. What kind of a world would it be? This isn't the Wild West. We don't live like that anymore. We have laws. When someone does something you don't like, you try to convince them to change their mind or you take them to court. You don't take the law into your own hands."

Zach hung his head. "I wrote Mr. Bowen and apologized."

Lucy gave Zach a sidelong glance filled with contempt. "Yeh, but you didn't sign the letter."

"You! Don't mix in," her dad told Lucy sternly. "I'll take care of this."

"But, Dad, they're blaming us for things he did," she protested. "He ruined everything!"

"Lucy," her dad said in a warning tone of voice. "Git!"

"Okay," she said, hurrying out of the kitchen.

"Is that true?" he asked, turning back to Zach.

Zach nodded. "I was afraid to," he admitted.

"An unsigned apology isn't an apology," his dad said. "Get out a piece of paper. You are going to write another letter to Mr. Bowen."

"But . . . but Dad, what about . . . the police?" Zach wailed.

"You should have thought about that before," his dad said grimly. He watched while Zach got his notebook and a pencil. Then he went to make some phone calls, leaving Zach sitting in front of a blank piece of paper.

Zach gripped the pencil tightly. He started to write the word *Dear*. The point broke and he flung the pencil across the room.

The music stopped in the other room. The piano lesson was over. Another minute and his mother would be on him too. Zach's eyes burned and his nose was running. His parents hated him. They were going to let him go to jail. They didn't care. Lucy hated him, too, and as soon as the other kids found out, everybody would hate him. The canyon would be developed and it was all his fault.

Zach got himself a tissue and wiped his eyes. He was blowing his nose when his brother came in. "What's going on?" Ben asked.

"Go away!" Zach grumbled.

"You're not the only one who lives here," said Ben. He opened the refrigerator and took out the apple juice. He took a glass from the drainer, poured some juice in it, and drank it. Then he went into the living room to watch the television.

Zach looked down at the piece of paper in front of him. He couldn't do it. He looked up at the clock and got up and went into the living room. "I need to see the news," he said, picking up the remote.

"Hey, I'm watching this," Ben protested.

"It's going to be over in a second," Zach said, switching the channel. He sat at the edge of the couch with his eyes riveted to the screen as Hap Townsend and Patti Flynn appeared. They reported on a tornado that killed eleven people in Texas, a hit-and-run accident in Vista that left a thirteen-year-old girl dead, and the murder of a seventy-nine-year-old woman in Oceanside. The news was almost over and Zach thought maybe he was in the clear when Hap Townsend said, "In a developing story, an eleven-year-old boy told our channel 8 reporter Judy Estrada that he was responsible for a recent rash of vandalism at the Bowen Corporation's San Ramon Canyon Development. We cannot name the boy because of his age, but he said he did it to save San Ramon Canyon from development. As yet, no charges have been filed."

"Hap, I understand the boy sent the Bowen Corporation his collection of baseball cards."

"Yes,Patti," Hap said. "He claims it was meant to pay for the damage. He's quoted as saying he was sorry that he didn't have more cards so he could buy the canyon and turn it into a park."

Patti Flynn shook her head sympathetically. "That's incredible, Hap. I don't know many kids who would give up their baseball cards for a park. Do you, Andy?" she asked turning to Andy Demko, the sportscaster.

"No," said Andy Demko. "I wouldn't have. I still have mine somewhere in my parents' garage. Maybe I should send them out to that kid in San Ramon so he can buy his park."

"Better take a look at them first. They may be worth a lot of money," said Hap Townsend.

"Did you hear what he said, Zach?" Ben asked excitedly as a picture of the weatherman standing in front of the cove at La Jolla appeared.

Zach nodded wearily. "He was just trying to be funny, Ben."

"So what? It's a great idea," Ben said.

"If you ask me, it's . . . ," Zach began, then, seeing his dad coming down the hall, he didn't finish.

"Did you write the letter I asked you to?" asked his dad.

"I was just watching the news. I'm going to do it right now."

"I want that letter done right after dinner," said his dad. He paused. "Your mom has the idea that you might not have been alone in this affair. Was Trevor or any of your other friends involved?"

Zach didn't answer.

"I see," his dad said quietly. "I think your loyalty might be misplaced. But I can't force you to name the other kids. You know this kind of behavior can't go unpunished, Zach. And you are going to be punished, you can be sure of that. To begin with, your mom and I want you home right after school every day, no matter what. I spoke to Dave Saperstein, our lawyer. He is writing a letter from your mother and me to the Bowen Corporation offering to pay the damages. And you, sonny boy, are going to pay us back every penny. We'll take it out of your allowance and in chores. There are a lot of things that need doing around here."

"But, Dad," Ben interrupted. "Zach already sent them his baseball cards."

His dad looked grim. "He can't prove that. Zach didn't sign the letter, did he?"

His dad's words kept echoing through Zach's mind all through dinner. How had he gotten himself into such trouble? All he and Trevor wanted to do was stop Bowen from taking away their canyon. How had it happened? He didn't want to think about it but he couldn't stop thinking about it. He knew it was wrong to pull up the stakes and he went ahead and did it anyway. Why? Because of Trevor? Because he was afraid of what Trevor would think? That was part of it, but only part.

The part that was hardest to admit even to himself was that he, Zach, had wanted to do it too, and he had let himself get carried away.

After dinner his dad sat with him at the kitchen table while he wrote another apology to Mr. Bowen. This time he signed his name, *Zachary James Barnes.*

CHAPTER 14

S INCE THE MEETING at the Silver Dragon, the Barnes
house had been flooded with petitions. As organizers of
Save San Ramon Canyon, the job of counting all the
names on the petitions had fallen to Zach, Lucy, and Ben.
Some afternoons friends came over to help, which made the
work go more quickly. But there were always more to be
counted after they left. Now, after a month, the petitions had
stopped coming in and they were almost finished counting.

"How many signatures so far?" Lucy asked.

Ben typed a command on the computer. "Ten thousand,
one hundred twenty-two."

"Hey, that's almost everybody in San Ramon," Lucy said.
"I'm calling city hall and asking the clerk to put us on the
agenda for the next council meeting."

Zach and Ben continued the tally. Lucy went to the
kitchen to make the call. A few minutes later she was back.
"We're on the agenda!" she said. Zach had always wondered

what "dancing with joy" meant; watching Lucy he thought he finally understood.

"The meeting is December ninth. We have to get the word out now, if we want a good turnout," Lucy continued. "Ben, you contact all the kids on the e-mail list. Zach, you call the first ten kids on our telephone list and ask them each to call ten other kids."

Zach and Ben snapped mock salutes, but Lucy ignored them. "I'm going to draft a flyer to hand out in front of the market. We have some money left over from the car wash that should cover the cost," she continued.

The next few days were a whirlwind of activity as Lucy, Ben, and Zach spread the word about the city council meeting.

They all assumed that Zach would be the one to present the petitions to the city council. But when Lucy asked Zach what he was going to say, Zach said he couldn't do it. "I can't be the spokesman for you guys. Remember, I'm the kid who vandalized Bowen's property. Nobody will listen to me."

"But the petition was your idea," said Ben.

Zach shook his head. "I'd ruin it for everybody," he insisted.

Ben turned to Lucy. "That leaves you."

Lucy looked stricken. "I'm not a good public speaker. I was awful at the Silver Dragon. Please don't make me do this."

"You have to, Lucy," Zach said. "You'll be okay. Remember to talk loud and go slow."

* * *

There was an air of excitement as people began to file into the San Ramon City Council chambers. Neighbors waved across the room to one another, friends stopped in the aisles to chat, people craned their necks to see who was behind them. The place was packed. All the seats were taken and people were milling in the aisles.

Just a few minutes before the meeting was to begin, the fire marshal announced that the aisles had to be cleared. "Take your seats," the custodian called to the people crowding the room.

"There aren't any seats left," a high school girl complained.

"You can't block the aisle," said the custodian. "You'll have to leave the room."

The girl didn't budge. "We have as much right to be here as anybody else," she insisted.

"Fire marshal's orders. You have to clear the aisles," the custodian repeated.

A murmur went through the crowd, then a male voice called out, "I'm not leaving until we give our petition to the council."

"Me either!" said a woman.

Soon everyone was talking at once. The janitor went to find the fire marshal, but he didn't have any success in moving the crowd out into the hallway either. The standoff lasted several minutes until Mayor Vasquez came to the front of the room and announced that he was having speakers put in the room next door so that those who couldn't find seats in the council chamber could hear the proceedings. Grumbling, the overflow crowd filed out of the council chamber. As they were leaving, Judy Estrada slipped by them and took a reserved seat in the front row.

The mayor banged his gavel, calling the meeting to order. The minutes from the previous meeting were read. There was a long discussion about whether or not the neighboring town of Seaside was within its rights putting parking meters on the north side of Valley Road.

"Wouldn't that depend on where the town line is?" a city councilwoman asked the city manager.

"That boundary is in dispute," the city manager replied.

Zach's mind wandered as the city manager explained the matter in tiresome detail. He snapped to attention when the council started discussing a contract with a trash hauling company, but soon lost interest. He listened with interest to the debate over whether there was a need for a traffic light at the corner of Valley and San Ramon Boulevard, until the traffic engineer began to talk about delay times for turning lanes. It was almost ten o'clock by the time Mayor Vasquez asked the city clerk if there was any new business. Zach was suddenly awake.

"Your Honor, the Save San Ramon Canyon Committee has a petition to present to the council," said the city clerk.

The mayor glanced at the clock. "Is it on the agenda?"

The clerk was looking down at some papers and she didn't answer immediately, making Zach's breath catch. Then she looked up and said, "Yes, Your Honor, they were put on the agenda."

"We're running late. Please limit your remarks to ten minutes," said the Mayor. "And I'm afraid we'll have to forgo questions."

The audience sounded like a swarm of angry bees. A voice from the back of the room shouted, "We've been sitting here patiently for more than two hours waiting for this and we're not forgoing anything!" Zach turned around in his seat to see Mr. Klapper standing up. His face was purple with anger.

The mayor and several council members whispered among themselves for half a minute, and then he said, "You can proceed, but we would appreciate it if you would keep it short."

Lucy stood up. "Yes, Your Honor," she said. She walked to the front of the room followed by four other kids who carried the boxes of signed petitions.

"Mayor Vasquez, members of the city council, I am speaking for the Save the Canyon Committee and the 10,387 residents of San Ramon who signed our petition," Lucy said. Her voice was clear and strong. "We respectfully ask that you reconsider your decision to give the Bowen Development Corporation a permit to build in San Ramon Canyon.

"San Ramon doesn't need more houses. It needs a park. We have a beautiful canyon in our city that everybody has used as a park for thirty years. The Bowen Development Corporation has closed it off. The U.S. Fish and Wildlife Service has already delayed the development until a plan is worked out to protect an endangered species that was found in the canyon. Now the majority of the citizens of San Ramon ask that you cancel the permit you gave the Bowen Corporation and offer to purchase the property for a park."

When Lucy finished there was thunderous applause. Mayor Vasquez put his hand up for quiet, but the crowd in the overflow room couldn't see him and they continued to whistle and cheer Lucy's speech for several minutes after she was done talking. The applause was so loud that the mayor had to wait until someone went next door to quiet them down.

Mayor Vasquez thanked Lucy. Then, turning to the audience, he said, "I think we need to back up here. The City approached the Bowen Development Corporation with an offer to buy several acres for a park in San Ramon Canyon some time ago." He turned to the clerk. "Do you remember when that was, Mrs. Matthews?"

Mrs. Matthews looked up. "Two years ago, Your Honor."

"At that time Bowen refused to consider the city's offer, which was their right," he continued. "The Bowen Corporation applied to the planning commission for a permit to develop that land, which was also their right. The permit was granted after exhaustive review, and in the absence of compelling legal reasons, we cannot rescind that permit. It is up to the U.S. Fish and Wildlife Service to decide if there is evidence of a negative environmental impact, not this council."

Several members of the city council nodded their heads, signaling their agreement with the mayor.

"I agree with you about the need for a public park, but given the lateness of the hour, we cannot take the matter up for discussion now. Mrs. Matthews, please place it on the agenda for another meeting," the Mayor said, bringing the meeting to a close.

With a scuffling of chairs, a few people got up to leave. Most of the audience sat in stunned silence. Then, as if waking from a dream, they began to file out.

The Barnes family was quiet on the drive home, except for Ben, who kept babbling about saving the canyon with baseball cards. Lucy snapped, "Shut up, Ben!" and started crying. "Don't you understand? The Bowen Corporation will start building as soon as the two hundred and forty day emergency listing is up. The government is on their side. Nobody is going to stop them for a mouse! We lost. It's over."

"But . . . but the man on television said . . . ," Ben sputtered miserably.

"But the man? The man is a sportscaster. He doesn't know anything about it, stupid!" Lucy shouted.

"Lucy, that's enough," Dad said sharply.

Mom reached over the seat and put her hand on Ben's knee to comfort him.

Zach stared out the window. Poor Ben, he thought sadly. Poor Lucy. Poor us. The petition didn't change a thing. Trevor was right about that.

CHAPTER 15

ZACH COULD BARELY DRAG himself out of bed the morning after the city council meeting. It took him forever to put on one of his shoes. The kitchen was empty, but *The San Ramon Blade* was lying on the table opened to page three. The headline said SAN RAMON CITY COUNCIL PASSES ON PETITION. Zach read it and dropped his head in his hands.

He got up from the table and left the house. He wished he didn't have to go to school and face everybody. Instead of heading down Canyon Road to school, he walked up the street past Trevor's house. It had been more than two weeks since he and Trevor had stopped walking to school together. He almost turned back to knock on Trevor's door but decided he couldn't bear to hear him say, "I told you so." He turned onto Crest Drive and found himself in front of Mr. Klapper's house. Suddenly it occurred to him that what he really wanted to do was to see the canyon. It would only take a few minutes. He paused, trying to decide whether or not to cut through Mr. Klapper's property when the side gate opened and Mr. Klapper came staggering out with a huge trash barrel overflowing with branches and clippings. Halfway down the driveway he had to put it down and drag it. Zach ran over and grabbed the other side to steady it.

"That was some meeting last night, eh?" Mr. Klapper said to him as they dragged the barrel down the driveway. "We should have known not to expect anything from those gutless wonders we elected to the city council. And the mayor is the worst of the lot."

Zach nodded. He couldn't believe he was having an actual conversation with Mr. Klapper!

Mr. Klapper continued, "It looks bad for the canyon. But as they say, "it ain't over till it's over. Who knows? We might still do an end run around them."

This was a side of Mr. Klapper Zach had never seen before, and it gave him the courage to ask him if he would let him cut through his backyard. Mr. Klapper said sure, and Zach followed him around the house to the back gate. He ran and slid halfway down the bluff, then stopped to drink it all in: the cool breeze on his arms; the smell of sagebrush; the dark green of the sumac and toyon bushes against the tan bluffs; the silvery thread of water at the bottom; and the slice of blue sky between the cliffs. This was where he and Trevor came to explore and to challenge themselves—this was where they had climbed and played and where he had gone into the cave and discovered bats.

Zach wrapped his arms around himself. He missed those times. He missed having a best friend to do things with. But did he miss Trevor? Sometimes. Would he and Trevor ever be friends again? It didn't seem likely now. But even if he and Trevor did make up, it would never be the same.

With a sigh, Zach turned around and made his way back up the bluff and down the road to school. It was going to be a long day.

Lucy and Ben were in the living room watching the six o'clock news on television when Zach came home from his clarinet lesson that afternoon. Watching the news seemed to have become a habit with them all, thought Zach. Well, not with him tonight. He started to walk by them, but Lucy stopped him. "Don't you want to see what they say about the city council meeting?"

Zach shrugged and slumped down on the couch beside his brother. He tossed a throw pillow in the air and caught it and tossed it again while Patti Flynn and Hap Townsend reported the usual bank robberies, car crashes, and fires. Then Judy Estrada appeared in front of the San Ramon City Hall and Zach dropped the pillow and leaned toward the screen.

"The San Ramon City Council was presented with a petition signed by two-thirds of that city's residents, asking them to revoke a building permit allowing the Bowen Development Corporation to develop San Ramon Canyon. This intensifies the pressure on Bowen Corporation to cancel plans to construct an exclusive gated community on the property. Six weeks ago, a colony of endangered pocket mice was found in the canyon, and the Bowen Corporation has already been prohibited from developing the land until it comes up with a plan to protect the mice. The council chamber was packed with supporters of the petition who were very upset when the mayor decided to put off discussion of the matter." The camera zoomed in on her serious expression before the scene switched back to the anchors in the studio.

"Is there any chance the council will revoke that permit, Judy?" Hap Townsend asked.

The scene switched back to Judy Estrada in San Ramon. "It doesn't seem likely, Hap. There are serious legal questions involved. Back to you, Patti."

"And now for the latest sports news, here's Andy Demko," said Patti Flynn.

As the anchorwoman's face was replaced by the sportscaster's, Ben pointed at the screen. "He's the one who said people should send you their baseball cards."

"He was just trying to . . ." Zach stopped in midsentence. The baseball cards could be just the end run Mr. Klapper was talking about! "Let's do it!" he said.

"Do what?" asked Lucy.

Ben grinned. "Get people to send us their old baseball cards so we can buy the canyon. Right, Zach?"

"Right," Zach said, slapping his brother on the back.

Lucy rolled her eyes. "You both are nuts. It won't work.

Do you think Mr. Bowen is going to give up his property for some old baseball cards after he refused to sell it to the city for money?"

"You never know. If enough people sent cards, he might change his mind," Zach countered.

"Listen!" said Ben. "We'll go on the Internet and ask people to send us their cards. There are lots of baseball card chat rooms and bulletin boards on the net."

Lucy got up from the couch. "Even if the Bowen Corporation would sell the land, no kid is going to give up his baseball cards just because you ask him to."

"We'll see," Zach said. "Lots of people like that sportscaster have old baseball cards sitting around out in their garages. I'll bet they'd be willing to give them up for a good cause—and we have one." The more he thought about it, the better he liked the idea.

The boys rushed through dinner and the dishes and ran to the computer in the den. Together they composed a message:

WANTED: BASEBALL CARDS!

If you have extra baseball cards, send them to us. We can use them to buy San Ramon Canyon and save it from becoming a housing development.

Lucy passed by the computer as they were writing the message. "You guys, nobody in their right mind is going to

130

buy this. They're going to think it's a trick so you can keep the cards yourself."

"She's right," Zach agreed. "We can't ask them to send the cards to us. We should tell them to send the cards directly to Mr. Bowen."

They corrected the message and typed the address of the Bowen Development Corporation at the bottom before sending it out over the Internet. In addition to baseball card collectors' newsgroups and chat rooms, they sent the message to everybody on their e-mail list and asked them to pass it on.

Zach went to sleep thinking about all the people all over California, all over the entire U.S.A., all over the world, reading their message and sending baseball cards to the Bowen Corporation. For the first time in weeks he slept through the night.

At school the next day, it seemed as if every free moment someone else was coming up to him to ask about the canyon. On the way home, he came up with another great idea. He would call Judy Estrada and ask her to put the baseball card campaign on the news. After all, they had channel 8 to thank for the inspiration.

Zach picked up the phone even before he took off his backpack. He had carried the card the reporter had given him ever since the meeting at the Silver Dragon. Now he pulled it out of his pocket and dialed the number under Judy Estrada's name. The phone rang. A cheery voice said, "Channel 8 Newsroom." Zach asked to speak to Judy Estrada in his most grown-up voice. The receptionist transferred the call. Judy Estrada's voice mail answered and Zach hung up.

Idiot! Zach thought. I should've left a message for her. He called back and left a message asking her to call him.

The phone was ringing as Zach and Ben walked in the door after school a few days later. Zach ran to answer it. It wasn't Judy Estrada, but it was a woman who asked to speak to Zachary Barnes.

"Speaking," he said.

"This is Sherri McInness from channel 8 news," the voice said. "I'm returning your call to Ms. Estrada. She apologizes for not getting back to you in person, but she's on assignment. I'm her assistant. Is it something I can help you with?"

"It's about sending . . ." Zach's voice trailed off. "Never mind." He hung up the phone.

"Who was it?" Ben asked.

"It was somebody calling back for Judy Estrada," said Zach.

"I thought you were going to tell her about our plan," said Ben.

"She wouldn't be interested."

"How do you know? You didn't tell her. Lots of people think it's a cool idea."

"I could just tell. She was trying to brush me off." Zach sighed wearily. "I was counting on her putting our plan on the news. Now we'll never get enough cards."

"Hey, never underestimate the power of the Internet!"

said Ben. He grabbed a banana from a bowl of fruit and went into the den.

Zach slipped off his backpack. He opened the refrigerator door and peered inside. There was nothing he wanted but his stomach felt empty. It made him mad that Judy Estrada had been nice to him when she thought she could get a story out of him, and now that the story was over, she was too busy to be bothered. He took a slice of bread out of the breadbox. He found the peanut butter in the pantry. He spread the peanut butter on the bread. I'll show her, he thought. Channel 8 news isn't the only news organization around.

"Hey, Ben," he called, putting the sandwich down uneaten. "Get off the computer! I'm going to write a letter to *The San Ramon Blade*."

The Blade printed Zach's letter four days later and several people responded, writing letters of their own, but Zach began to feel as if nothing he did made a difference. The fate of the canyon seemed sealed. He had just about given up hope when Grandpa Al called from Phoenix, Arizona. Zach was about to call his mom to the phone when his grandfather stopped him.

"Hold on there," he said. "I want to talk to you. What's the name of that canyon near the house?"

"San Ramon," said Zach. "Why do you want to know, Grandpa?"

"I told you it was San Ramon Canyon," his grandfather

shouted to someone in the background. "Zach, have you heard about those kids who are trying to buy the canyon with baseball cards? One of the guys I play golf with was telling me he read about it in the newspaper. I thought you might know about it."

"Ben and I—we started it," Zach said.

Grandpa Al laughed appreciatively. "Well, you've made the national news. Here, let me read you the article:"

BASEBALL CARDS OFFERED FOR CANYON

Children in San Ramon, California, are hoping to trade their baseball cards for a canyon. They have sent hundreds of boxes of the trading cards to the Bowen Development Corporation, owner of San Ramon Canyon, in a drive to buy the land and stop the development of luxury homes there.

The children have used word of mouth, e-mail, and letters to the editor to convince others to join them in their drive. Their goal is to have the canyon declared a public park.

But the Bowen Development Corporation refuses to trade. A spokesman said that the corporation is proceeding with its plans.

Development was halted this fall when 39 rare Pacific pocket mice were discovered nesting in the canyon. The mice have been placed on the emergency endangered species list. Under the listing, the corporation has 240 days to submit a plan that will ensure that the development will not further endanger the rare mouse.

"What's happening?" Lucy asked, coming into the kitchen.

"It's Grandpa. He read about us in the Phoenix newspaper," Zach said.

"That reminds me," said Lucy. "I keep forgetting to tell you. Lots of kids have been coming up to me at school and telling me they're sending their baseball cards to Bowen. There's this girl in my class who desperately wants to be cool. Her name is Courtney and she's actually buying baseball cards to send to Bowen. Now let me talk to Grandpa."

A few days later, Mike Barnes brought a copy of *The San Diego Chronicle* home from the office. On the back page was a picture of the San Ramon post office with stacks of boxes everywhere. It read:

BASEBALL CARD DRIVE FLOODS
SAN RAMON POST OFFICE

It was a scene from *Miracle on Thirty-fourth Street,* but instead of letters to Santa, the tiny San Ramon post office was flooded with boxes of baseball trading cards all addressed to the Bowen Development Corporation.

A spokesman for Bowen announced Monday that the company no longer will accept unsolicited packages and the mail has been piling up at the post office ever since.

Bowen has been inundated with boxes of baseball trading cards in recent weeks, some coming from as far away as Augusta, Maine. The baseball cards are part of a campaign waged by local children to save San Ramon Canyon from development and turn it into a park. The post office refused to comment on the situation.

The Bowen Corporation plans to build 95 luxury homes in the canyon later this year.

Zach was outraged. "They can't do that!" he cried when he read the story. "It wrecks everything."

"You may have met your match, sonny boy," said Zach's dad. "These corporations know all the tricks and they aren't afraid to use them. But we're still proud of you for trying."

Zach's mom put her hand on his shoulder. "Lord knows, you have been persistent, Zach. You kept on trying when everybody else gave up. It takes lots of courage to do that and I admire you for it."

Zach's heart swelled. They didn't think he was the worst kid in the world after all!

CHAPTER 16

CHRISTMAS CAME AND went. So did Martin Luther King Day and Presidents' Day. It was April. In San Ramon Canyon, wildflowers were blooming on the bluffs. Birds were chirping and twittering in the bushes. Tadpoles were hatching in the creek and baby rabbits were bounding out from under bushes, freezing, and darting for cover again. But it had been so long since the people of San Ramon had been able to enjoy the beauty of the canyon, they were beginning to forget that it was there.

Zach and Ben had stopped sending out messages on the Internet and reminding everybody to send their baseball cards to the Bowen Corporation right after the post office stopped delivering the packages. The city council had yet to schedule the public park discussion. As time passed and nothing new happened, Zach grew worried. He needed to find something to keep everybody interested in the canyon. But what?

He couldn't think of anything to do until one day when he was flipping through the family section of the newspaper and saw an announcement for another photography contest. That was it! He would take pictures of the canyon in bloom. The pictures would appear in the newspaper and everybody would want to go to the canyon. When they remembered that they couldn't get there, they would become angry and look for ways to change the situation.

Zach felt shy about calling Mr. Klapper to ask if he could cut through his yard. Instead, he walked by his house on Monday when he knew Mr. Klapper would be carrying out the trash. The trash was already sitting at the curb when he got there. Zach was afraid that if he went up to the door, Rogue would go crazy barking. He turned around and started walking back down the hill and then stopped. This was ridiculous; he was brave enough to take on the Bowen Corporation. Why was he afraid to knock on a door? He turned and walked up to the door and knocked. Rogue barked. He heard Mr. Klapper say, "Shh! Rogue!" and the door opened. "It's you, Zach," Mr. Klapper said, almost as if he was happy to see him. "Come on in."

Zach shook his head. "I can't now. I have to get to school. But I want to take some pictures of the canyon this afternoon to send to *The Blade* for their photo contest. I just don't want people to forget it's here. Can I come through your yard about three o'clock?"

Mr. Klapper smiled. "Of course you can," he said. "I love being a thorn in the side of that old money-sack Bowen. Just knock before you go around back so I can put Rogue in the house."

Zach smiled to himself as he headed back down the hill. It was funny how things turned out. Six months ago he would have sworn he and Trevor would be friends for life and that never in a million years would he talk to Old Man Klapper. Sometimes Trevor and he found themselves walking to school at the same time and even talked now and then, but nowadays he spent more time with Brian and Robert. And as for Mr. Klapper, who would have guessed?

That afternoon there was an express mail envelope waiting for Zach when he got home from school. "Who's it from?" Lucy wanted to know.

Zach looked at the return address. "It's from the Bowen Development Corporation. I don't want to open it. You do it," he said, handing the envelope to his sister. He held his breath while she tore open the envelope and pulled out a single piece of paper. "It's a press release. They're having a press conference at noon tomorrow at the Bowen Corporation's headquarters. There's a handwritten note on the bottom that says, 'Zachary, I hope you and your family can make it. Come a few minutes early so we can talk. Raymond Bowen.'"

Zach was puzzled. Why would Mr. Bowen want him at a

press conference? The invitation was probably a trick so they could arrest him for vandalism. They hadn't forgiven him. Not Mr. Bowen and his corporation. Not his mother. Not his father. And not even Zach himself. He would remember what he and Trevor had done with shame for as long as he lived. "I'm not going," he said.

"Why?" Lucy asked. "Mr. Bowen went out of his way to invite you."

"I'm not going," he repeated stubbornly.

"But you can't miss this. They wouldn't invite you if there wasn't going to be some big announcement. It doesn't matter if it's good news or bad news, somebody from the Save San Ramon Canyon committee should be there."

"You go. I'm not going."

"I don't understand. Why won't you go?" Lucy said. "I'm telling Mom about this."

His mom guessed what was bothering him right away. "It's the vandalism, isn't it, Zach? You know you are not going to be arrested. You have to understand that your life isn't over because you made a mistake. You admitted it. You tried to make it right. You can't ever make it go away, but you did what you could. And now you have to move on."

"Okay, I'll go to their press conference," Zach agreed reluctantly. "But only if all of you come with me."

Mrs. Barnes wrote notes asking that her children be excused from school early for the press conference. She made

Lucy wear a skirt and the boys wear dress shirts and slacks to school. Zach felt as if everybody was staring at him all morning. Mom came to pick him and Ben up at 11:30. "Dad's going to bring Lucy as soon as he gets out of his meeting," she said, leading the way to the car.

It didn't take long to reach the headquarters of the Bowen Development Corporation. Zach hesitated on the wide marble steps in front of the big glass building. He felt like the guy in the movies who walks unarmed into the enemy camp. Everybody knew what happened to that guy.

"Are you coming?" his mom said, turning around and waiting for Zach to catch up. He cringed when they told the receptionist who they were, but all she said was, "Take the elevator to the top floor. Mr. Bowen is expecting you."

The ride to the top floor seemed much too quick. The elevator door opened into another lobby where an efficient-looking woman was sitting behind a huge desk. "Would you mind waiting here for a moment?" she said with a smile. "Mr. Bowen is on the telephone."

After a few minutes, the large door behind the receptionist opened and a tall, important-looking white-haired man stepped out and came toward them with his hand extended. He had a down-curved nose like a hawk's beak. "Sorry to keep you waiting," he said. "You must be Mrs. Barnes." He shook her hand. Then, looking at Zach, "This must be my adversary, Zachary." He held his hand out to Zach and Zach remembered to shake it. "And who is this?" he asked, looking down at Ben.

"Benjamin Gabriel Barnes, another adversary," Ben said, holding his hand out for Mr. Bowen to shake.

"I'm happy to meet two such worthy opponents," said Mr. Bowen, leading them into an office three times the size of the Barneses' living room. He offered Mrs. Barnes a cup of coffee and Ben and Zach sodas. Zach relaxed a little. Mr. Bowen wouldn't offer him a soda if he was going to have him arrested, would he?

Mr. Bowen took a seat in an armchair across from them. "Your letter made a strong impression on me, Zachary. It takes courage to admit you've made a mistake and more courage to try to right it. It made me think that maybe I'd made a mistake, too.

"What came through in both your letters was your love for the canyon. Magic, you called it. Then there was this out-pouring of baseball cards, which my grandson says you boys started. It's unbelievable how many people have sent us their baseball trading cards. People who have never seen the canyon sent letters urging us not to develop it. So I decided I'd better see what all the fuss was about. I went down to see the canyon for myself. I'm ashamed to admit it's been years since I've been down there. I forgot how beautiful it is. That's what clinched it for me. I would have to be the meanest, greediest person alive not to share that beauty with others."

He's not going to build, Zach realized. But it seemed too good to be true. There had to be a catch.

Mr. Bowen looked at his watch and stood up. "It's time to go downstairs. Mayor Vasquez and the press will be waiting." He ushered them to the elevator.

"Either of you boys play baseball, or do you just collect the cards?" Mr. Bowen asked, making conversation on the way down in the elevator. Zach decided it would be safest to say as little as possible, but as usual, Ben couldn't keep quiet.

"I'm in Little League. I play second base," he said.

"That was my position. Hard to believe it now, but I was quite a baseball player in my day. I even made it into the minor leagues," Mr. Bowen said.

"But not the majors?" Ben asked.

Mr. Bowen shook his head. "I hurt my shoulder my first season and that was the end of my baseball career. But I've been a fan ever since."

Ben started to ask him what team he'd played for, but he didn't have a chance before the elevator doors opened and they were in a hall leading to a big room filled with people.

"I want you to sit up here with me," Mr. Bowen said to Zach, guiding him to the front of the room. They sat down next to the mayor, whom Zach recognized from the city council meeting. Zach looked out over the audience. His dad and Lucy were there, settling into seats in the front next to

Mom and Ben. So was Judy Estrada. She was sitting on the end of a row, near the back of the room.

The mayor was the first to speak. "On behalf of the City of San Ramon, I am pleased to announce that the Bowen Development Corporation has donated sixty-five acres of San Ramon Canyon to the city for use as a city park and nature preserve. It is an enormous gift to the city and to its residents." Everyone applauded.

Turning toward Mr. Bowen, he continued. "I wish to express our gratitude to Ray Bowen and to the Bowen Development Corporation for their generosity, civicmindedness, and farsightedness. Their gift to the city will make San Ramon an even more attractive community to live in than it already is. It gives our residents a beautiful place where they can get away from the pressures of their everyday lives. Most important, it preserves a natural treasure for the enjoyment of future generations." Everyone applauded again.

The mayor sat down and Mr. Bowen stood up. "I have seen San Ramon grow from a few houses on a dusty ranch into a small model city and I am very proud of the part I've played in its development. But I am even prouder to be able to give something of value back to this community."

He put his hand on Zach's shoulder. "This is Zachary Barnes. Zach is the one who made me change my mind about the canyon. Stand up, Zachary, so everybody can see you."

Zach stood up slowly. Everybody clapped and Zach's ears

turned red with embarrassment.

"I can tell you it's no joke to have this boy as your adversary." Everybody laughed. "I still don't know how he managed to find that pocket mouse and take its picture. He started a petition to save the canyon and, when that effort failed, he turned to the Internet, newspapers, and every other means of communication to ask people to send us their baseball cards. I have no idea what he was going to come up with next, but I have no doubt he had something up his sleeve. I tell you, this kid doesn't give up. You might say that our plans for San Ramon Canyon were buried under an avalanche of baseball cards."

"And a pocket mouse," someone called out from the audience. It sounded suspiciously like Charles Klapper Jr. and Zach searched the crowd and saw both Klappers, father and son, sitting three rows from the front.

"And a pocket mouse," Mr. Bowen agreed, smiling. "One of the things you learn when you run a business is how to compromise. A nature preserve for the Pacific pocket mouse within the public park is part of the agreement we have worked out with the U.S. Fish and Wildlife Service. And this compromise allows the Bowen Corporation to develop the remaining fifty-four acres of the canyon. The park will have trails for jogging and hiking, as well as a baseball diamond, playground, and picnic area for all of us in San Ramon to enjoy."

Mr. Bowen turned to Zach. "What do you say to that, Zachary? Does that sound all right to you?"

"All right?" said Zach. "Of course it's all right! All we ever wanted was to have our canyon back and now we've got that and more."